Flying High,

Diving Deep

BarbarianSpy

FOR LITERARY HEAT

www.BarbarianSpy.com

This book is copyright © habu 2012
Published by BarbarianSpy in 2012
Cover design © S Bush 2012
Cover image: © Les3photo8 | Dreamstime.com
ISBN 978-1-921879-30-2
All rights reserved

Flying High, Diving Deep

A Factional Memoir
of the Gay Life of habu

habu

Table of Contents

Introduction

Flying High, Diving Deep provides a three-decade memoir of the gay portion of a male bisexual's awakening to, nearly unfettered enjoyment of, and sometimes bittersweet reflections on the active gay lifestyle on the international scene in the latter third of the twentieth century. The author was a male model and film actor who turned to international intelligence service during the latter Vietnam War era, a career that started off in the stratosphere as an SR71 photoreconnaissance jet pilot and moved on to more earth-hugging intelligence and diplomatic service in Asia and the Middle East.

Although coming late—in his late twenties—to the gay scene, the author's sexual encounters and experience as a willing bottom blossomed quickly in the exotic, sexually free, risk-taking, and pre-AIDS environment of Bangkok, Thailand. *Flying High, Diving Deep* covers the high points of the author's sexual experiences in twenty-five short stories that are chronologically laid out. They take the reader from the author's male-male initiation in Bangkok in the mid 70s through gay sexual encounters during stints in Japan and the Middle East to the concluding years of the last decade of the twentieth century as he thought his gay life activity was waning, only to be joyfully reawakened. The author provides a no-holds-barred, insightful, and never shirking from bittersweet remembrances series of snapshots that move from the free, sensual, "anything goes" international gay scene through the realities of the horror of AIDS to appreciation for the deep, lasting relationships that arise from the world of men loving men.

The first fifteen vignettes are set in Bangkok in the mid 70s, where the author is first made aware of his gay interests and is initiated by a masterful Egyptian predator of young men ("Egyptian Initiation"), introduced into threesome sex by his teacher ("First Threesome"), and then turned over to a more demanding lover ("Israeli Assault"). Thereafter the author strikes out on his own, with encounters with his masseur ("Kasem's Kitchen"), party group sex ("The Cast Party"), and his ultimate lover ("Ten Slash Two"; immediately followed by "Power of the Major Emphasized," lest the reader not fully grasp the depth of this relationship; and, later in the memoir, "The Darling"). "The Golden Triangle" takes a peek, in story form, into how the author's bisexual interests were used by U.S. intelligence in Southeast Asia, and "Legend of Cowboy," "Family Day on the Pool Table," and "Double Bets" provide a sense of the wide-open sexual environment of Bangkok in the 1970s.

The latter part of this first set of vignettes moves the author from the 70s to the 80s and reveals the changing environment on the international gay scene, as the dangers of a hedonistic lifestyle and the complexity of male-male relationships begin to come home to roost. "Director's Couch" provides a glimpse into the film career life of the author, which overlapped his early intelligence service. "That One Exception" is a bittersweet love story giving insight into the capability of one man to love another, while "Rude Awakening" openly deals with the onset of the AIDS crisis and the realization of the need to use safe sex practices. The closing story of this section provides a glimpse into an interlude of an assignment to Okinawa, Japan, in the closing months of the author's life as a jet pilot.

The author spent the 80s through the early 90s in both the Middle East, with brief visits back to his family's ranch in the U.S. West, where his full-blown gay world side life is painted through the next set of vignettes. "The Ethiopian Cabin Boy" provides

8

another glimpse into how his lifestyle melded with the needs of his intelligence work, whereas "The Norwegian Stallion," "Turkish Delight Times Six," and "Someday My Prince Will . . ." entertain with the full-out sensuality of his life as a diplomat on the island of Cyprus. (This period is also illuminated by the separately published novella, *Platres Conclave.*) "Ride 'Em Cowboy" gives a stateside interlude to the delights to be had in the mountains of Colorado.

The last set of stories reflect the satisfying afterglow of renewed male-male sexual activity in the first decade of the twenty-first century following an interlude of several years in which the author assumed the active gay side of his sex life was over. "Renewal of Passion" and "At the Reservoir" paint this return to sexual encounters with men, while "Like Father Like Son" and "Uncertain Arrival" complete a circle back to men and satisfying relationships from the author's past, providing a satiating and memory-enhancing "autumn" glow for fully lived life on the fringe.

Chapter One: Egyptian Initiation

I now understand that my subconscious was miles ahead of my "surface" brain on knowing what I wanted. Male models apparently are as justly characterized as thick brained as female models are reputed to be. There was no blame to cast; I'd seen the Egyptian doctor (if he really was a doctor) work the young men on the gym floor and in the shower room. There was no reason my surface brain wouldn't know he was a sexual predator. In the end, I'm really glad it happened, though.

The Egyptian was a magician really—and I was the world's worst dummy. The first encounter happened without me having a clue about what had happened even when it was over. I was a few years older than those the Egyptian was targeting at the gym—and he was a good twenty years older than I was. He touched me in the sauna, and my cock burbled out juice without warning and certainly without my really realizing we were having any form of sex. He had a mesmerizing voice, and I got horny without the usual arousal mechanisms—no warning really. He was doing this monologue about being circumcised or not in those doctor words of his, as if we were having an academic discussion or a medical consultation, and he had his long, thin fingers on my cock head before I really knew what he was doing. I was so surprised that I shot right off. I was greatly embarrassed, thinking I had probably misjudged his intent and now he'd think I was queer. I left the sauna in a highly confused state.

For his part, he probably just thought I was performing a hard-to-get mating dance. I hadn't clocked him when he got hold of my cock. I'd just sat there and stared dumbly.

I stewed about the encounter for a week, and although I didn't think I was attracted to Egyptians, this one was quite handsome and distinguished and sensual looking. The next time we were in the sauna alone, I more or less set myself up for the pass, thinking he probably wouldn't even make one and I could put my confusion to rest. I stretched out on my back, towel loosely around my waist and stretching down to my knees. He came in and sat on the bench below me and beyond my feet. In somewhat of a trembling condition, I spread my thighs so that from where he was sitting, he could see up under my towel and check out the goods (if he wanted to). He obviously wanted to and liked what he saw.

An electric jolt went through me and I suddenly knew we were "doing something," when I felt his strong, long fingers on my foot and he was massaging it—the sole and the toes—and slowly pulling on toes in a sensual way. I went hard. He slowly worked his hand up my calf and knee and under the hem of the towel. That's when he started murmuring to me how nice my body was—and I was narcissistic enough to melt to his seduction. He'd seen me work out on the gym floor, he said, and he knew I was in TV commercials. His hand slowly went up the inside of my thigh and he was lightly stroking my cock. I shoot off almost immediately again. And, thick lunkhead that I was, I apologized for reacting sexually—when what I really was apologizing for was an early ejaculation. This hadn't happened to me with women. Obviously the new experience with men was just that much more arousing.

Still holding my cock, he said he could teach me some techniques that would help with that problem—he was talking like a doctor and like it would be something I could use with the women I was with. I weakly said I didn't have a problem with women, but I was talking pretty weakly because my attention was

12

riveted to what he was doing with his hand. He was palming my cock and stroking the pisshole with a thumb, rubbing my ejaculated cum around the head. He was still talking clinically enough that I was fooling myself a bit about what was going on. I said I'd think about it.

The next week, he overheard me being told that my regular masseur wouldn't be there that afternoon—I always worked out, showered, and then was rubbed down. The Egyptian then asked me while we were still out on the floor exercising whether I'd like to come back to his apartment after we worked out and he'd give me the massage I was missing. I was all aflutter, still not positive where this was leading, when we got to his place. He did have a massage room with a padded table and all. And he massaged my back and legs and arms with oil—doing a better job than my regular masseur did. He told me to roll over on my back, and when I did so, I saw that he now was naked. He was tall and lithe, but very well muscled, and he had a thin but very long dong. It wasn't hard at all, so I rationalized that I was pretty safe.

He was massaging my front with oil and my cock was standing up straight—and I was very embarrassed, not being able to control it and still figuring there was an outside chance he wasn't trying to do me, that this was all a misunderstanding on my part. When he got to my pelvis, he took possession of my cock with his hand and slowly jerked me off. I made some embarrassed comments about being sorry I'd gotten hard, and he could just try to ignore that, but he was soothing me with words to the effect that the Egyptian massage method included an "evacuation of the pent-up essences" and it was all very normal in the Egyptian context. But even then he was starting to teach me control. He'd pump me up and then hold off until I cooled. My cock and his hands were so oiled that there was little friction at all in what he was doing. At last he let me ejaculate and cleaned it up with a towel. He then massaged all of the muscles on my front side real well again and I got drowsy.

He came around to above my head and he was massaging my temples and really putting me to sleep. He put his hands on my upper sides and pulled me up on the table until my head dropped off the end of the table and he was still working my temples. Then I felt his cock at my lips and he was pushing in, suddenly very hard. I was shocked because he had hardened up almost instantaneously (something I later learned was in his bag of tricks). He didn't push far in, but I sort of spit it out and told him, rather frightened, that I'd never sucked a man before—that, in fact, I'd never had any form of sex with a man until now.

He went all impressed and joyful at the news that he had a virgin on his hands. While I had been wondering what was going on, he must have just thought I was into a foreplay game. He asked me if I'd let him initiate me. He begged me to let him prepare me for future encounters. He entreated me that I'd never have anyone as gentle and skilled as him if I had any inkling I wanted to be with men. He flattered me by wondering how anyone who looked like me could have gotten this far without going bi. He showed me a picture of his wife (it really was his wife, I found out later) and assured me that many men took pleasure both ways. Something inside me told me I didn't want to deny myself any opportunities to full sensuality, and I gulped and asked him if he really would be gentle. (I didn't think to ask him why I wasn't going to be fucking him instead, if I was all that hot.) To prove he would be gentle and careful, his cock did go back into my mouth, but only a little ways, and rotated around. He said we wouldn't have to get much into that for now. (My guess is that he wanted to get his dick up my ass before I thought better of the situation.)

He sent me off with an enema bottle then, saying I'd be more comfortable if I was cleaned out—and he went off to take a ritualistic shower (he said). He didn't want me to take a shower, I guess, because he wanted to roll around in the oil I'd been basted in.

When I came back, he had me go up on my belly on the table—I was oiled up so well now I could have slid off the table. I assumed he'd suck me off to show me how that was done, but he obviously was going straight for the main event. A virgin is a virgin. An American male model virgin in the grasp is probably a trip to paradise for an Egyptian. He put a pretty bulky pillow under my belly to lift my pelvis up. He then got up on the table, pushed my thighs wide, got down behind me, and tongued my asshole for a while. His tongue also went to the underside of my cock and around my balls and across my inner thighs in this process.

All the time he was telling me how nice I was and assuring me that I was slowly opening and that I'd be well open before he mounted me. He was pretty good at his word on that. He patiently worked on me for an hour or more (during which I shot off a couple more times, with his encouragement and clucking that I had nothing to be embarrassed about—I could reload within twenty minutes in those days and shoot off five or six times a night when I was really aroused). Varieties of lubricant were applied, some of which was for deadening the area (and probably was illegal). After his tongue, he went to fingers. He had long, sensual ones, and he could easily reach my prostate and show me how he could make me shoot off just by rubbing me there. Then well-oiled fingers probing deeper. Whatever he was using to deaden pain was only used on the rim and just a few inches inside, so he could be in a couple of inches before I even knew I was being skewered. He showed me a couple of smallish dildos of increasing size before he lubed them up and screwed them into my ass and around. Not much pain in any of this, and I was jacked up to the roof at the very idea of what was happening to me—the sheer risk and adventure of it—and the fact that I'd finally been brave enough to give it a try.

After more than an hour, I felt his cock at my back door, and he very slowly entered me—and entered me and entered me and entered me. That was one long cock. It felt like the uncoiling of a snake inside me. He had one of those "bent up" cocks too, so I could feel the head dragging along my ass canal walls as it plowed up me. There was some pain now, but I'm sure minimal pain for a first time. I'd been as gently prepared as I could wish for. He rode me, slowly pumping me deep, for a good thirty minutes, drawing out his pleasure with the virgin as much as he could, I suppose. He was braced on his knees behind me and either kept his hands hooked over my shoulders or palmed flat on my shoulder blades as his cock worked me. He was chattering away in his singsong voice, no doubt keeping me calm and mesmerized, and I could tell that the experience was quite arousing for him too, because he came quickly (for him—he was the master of self-control). His ejaculation felt like a warm oozing inside me, sort of a foreign tickling sensation.

He held there for a while, his cock buried to the hilt, massaging my muscles again and telling me what a lovely young man I was. I felt him go tumescent inside me. But he just kept massaging me, not letting me up. And I felt him start to engorge and fill up my ass canal again. I didn't feel sore inside, but the deadening was wearing off on the rim of my ass, and I felt a little chaffed there. It was obvious that he wasn't going to let the virgin get away with one screwing.

He pulled out of me and walked down the table on his knees, pulling me with him, until we were both standing on the floor at the edge of the table. Then he bent me over, my chest on the table, my legs wide, and he folded himself over me as well and slowly entered me a second time. This time I felt some pain at the entry and let him know he was hurting me. He shushed me like one would do a fussy baby and just kept plowing up my channel. He said he wanted briefly to let me feel another type of fucking and that he knew I'd enjoy it. He squeezed my thighs with his, which tightened my canal around his cock, and then he took me in long strokes, nearly all the way out, and then all the way back in. He did me for about fifteen minutes this way, and I was very vocal with this one, arching my back up to him and writhing my hips around. This is where I first experienced pain mixed so heavily with pleasure that I both was yelling that he was hurting me and pleading with him to keep pumping me. He claimed to really like my reaction to that position—and chose to keep pumping me.

Then he turned me on his cock, while pushing on my back onto the massage table. He spread my legs, and, saying this was yet another style I might like, he gave me a mixed-routine fuck. He'd pump me from the front with fast shallow strokes for five minutes, then he'd take the root of his cock in his hand and rotate it around inside me, hitting all the walls with that bent knob of his.

Then back to the short, fast strokes. I did a good bit of grunting and moaning for him in this position—and wondering if it was going to ever stop—not at all sure I wanted it to. He went deep then for about three plunges and he had cum again.

We showered together and that's when he went down in front of me in the cascading water and sucked me off. He did it quickly that afternoon. In later sessions he showed me he could drive me wild with his tongue and mouth work on my cock.

After drying off, he took me to his bed, and after lubing up my hole and his cock, he fucked me again in a side split—me on my left side, he on his left side behind and under me, his left arm under and around me, with his palm fanned out over my belly, his right hand holding my right leg up in the air, and his cock stroking up into me from behind and below. During this, he started showing me that men could exchange sensual kisses. After he was done with me in that position, I was exhausted and slept in his arms for over an hour, with his cock up my (now throbbing and sore) ass.

So, it took me a hell of a long time to get around to any "firsts," but then my real first was a doozy.

The Egyptian gave me ointments and lubricants to cut down on the "getting used to it" pain, and a collection of ever-larger butt plugs—that didn't stretch the rim too much, but that stretched the first three or four inches inside, so that big cocks could get in and not do too much damage.

Good thing I had this preparation and the first encounter/training I had with the sensitive Egyptian, because about six weeks after that, I was trapped in a massage room at the gym by a Swede with a thick good eight incher and was taken roughly and in no uncertain terms and little choice in the matter. (Of course, it was all my fault as I had purposely given him a good look at me and acted a little provocatively in the shower room to check out my effect on other men.) With the preparation the Egyptian "doctor" was giving me, I actually enjoyed the Swede.

Chapter Two: First Threesome

My first, memorable threesome was in that fancy gym in Bangkok where I had recently met the one I called my Egyptian magician, who had seduced and initiated me. And the threesome was orchestrated by that Egyptian diplomat as well. He had been eyeing a military attaché from the Israeli embassy on the exercise floor—a man pushing his forties, built close to the ground but with long arms, almost simian in appearance but not unattractive. Ropy muscles, swarthy, quite hirsute, particularly strong-looking legs, arms, and pecs, some interesting battle scars that made him distinctive in a dangerous, mysterious sort of way. He practiced a lot on the rings, and the way his muscles bulged during these exercises was very attracting.

The Egyptian propositioned the Israeli late one evening, who in turn said the one he really had his eye on at the gym was me. The Egyptian said I held myself aloof, but that he had had me, and if the Israeli arranged with the management for the three of us to stay past closing (which was a common occurrence at that gym—it was a male-male pickup joint), the Egyptian thought he could loosen me up for an approach by the Israeli, if the Israeli would accept a threesome. The Egyptian didn't really tell me any of this until after the fact.

The Egyptian and I were in the sauna, and he was kissing me and playing with my nipples with his hands, in preparation, I thought, for another massage treatment at his house later to end in a fuck. He was quite lithe and limber—not to mention inventive—that Egyptian, and I'd already become addicted to what his long, rather thin cock could do to me. The Israeli entered the sauna and sat on the bench across, but not too far away, from us. I thought the Egyptian would break away from me then, as he usually did when another man entered the sauna. But he kept on kissing me, and his hand went to rubbing my cock through the towel I had around my waist.

The Israeli was watching us intently, and when the Egyptian's lips left mine and moved down to my nipples and I arched my chest back for him, I saw the Israeli rubbing his own cock through his towel as well. Off came my towel, and the Egyptian was stroking my cock with his hand. Off came the Israeli's towel also, and I could see he had a hard on. The Egyptian stroked me and the Israeli stroked himself. His cock was a normal size, but it was heavily veined and had a nice big mushroom head on it. He was running his free hand around on his hairy chest, pinching at his nipples. His eyes held mine and I could see how badly he wanted me.

It wasn't long until he was sitting beside us. I had the Egyptian on one side and the Israeli on the other. The Israeli was kissing me and had a hand wrapped around my cock, and the Egyptian was running a hand between my chest and the chest and lap of the Israeli. It wasn't long before I had an engorged cock in each hand.

The Israeli kissed his way down my torso and into my lap, while the Egyptian was kissing me on the mouth. I felt the Israeli's lips on the head of my cock, but the Egyptian spoke then, suggesting that we needed to get out of the hot sauna and that we could continue under the water in the shower.

Shortly thereafter, we were under a light shower of water, the Israeli kneeling in front of me, working my cock with his mouth, and the Egyptian kneeling behind me, working my ass with his tongue. This went on until I had cum for the Israeli, Meanwhile, the Egyptian had my asshole opened wide and wet. The Egyptian stood and moved away from us, watching, as the

Israeli also stood and turned me toward the tiled wall, moist and slippery from the water running down it from the shower. His pelvis was planted in my rump, with his hard cock pushing at the small of my back. His arms were wrapped around my torso, with his fingers digging into my nipples. He was kissing my neck and whispering to me how beautiful my body was. He was polite enough to ask me if he could fuck me. And I was aroused enough to tell him he could.

He got his powerful thighs between mine and practically lifted my legs off the floor. One hand left my chest to help guide his cock. And I felt him at the hole the Egyptian had prepared from him. I turned my head and his lips possessed mine. I could see the Egyptian go down on his knees behind the Israeli. The Israeli was rimming my asshole with that mushroom head of his and then, with a long intake of breath, he started entering me. His tongue went wild in my mouth, as his cock forced its way up my ass canal. I stood on my tip toes and widened my access as much as I could for him. His cock wasn't as long as the Egyptian's was, but it was a little thicker. I was able to manage him in to the hilt, though, with little pain. His hands glided up my arms then, which he forced over my head, and he held my wrists against the wet tiles and pumped his dick up into me in long strokes. All the time he was telling me how nice my body—particularly my ass—was, which was just what I wanted to hear. He got so carried away that the Hebrew started fighting with the English for attention, but I thought it was nice to be having my body praised in another language.

He gave a little grunt and a cry out and his cock lurched inside me. I looked around and realized that the Egyptian was standing behind and hunched over the Israeli and fucking him. The Israeli shot off inside me almost immediately then but held me there, close to the tiled wall, with his body covering mine until the Egyptian was finished fucking him.

We all kissed and showered off and the Egyptian did take me home then to give me a good massage—and fuck me again in the leisure of his bedroom.

Chapter Three: Israeli Assault

I'll always remember the Israeli by the image of him standing there at the window of the Oriental Hotel room, the strong Bangkok sun bathing his body in afternoon light—that and by the cockiness with which he took control.

The Israeli army officer, a military attaché at his country's embassy in Thailand, had just two weeks earlier been part of my first threesome. He had seen me working out in the gym, and my Egyptian sexual mentor had said the Israeli could have me if he would agree to a threesome with the Egyptian. The Israeli must have been pleased by me, because the very next day he started a campaign to get me alone. He had begged and pleaded with me and had declared that he'd treat me like a priceless gift, and I had finally agreed to meet with him alone.

I was attracted to him, so the decision was not a hard one to reach. He was intriguing, almost simian in appearance, but in an attracting way. Somewhere in his early forties, but a magnificently maintained early forties, he was quite hairy, my first experience with anyone so heavily pelted, but also very muscular, and with arms longer in proportion to the rest of his body than normal. There had been nothing spectacular in the length and girth of his cock, but he had used it quite masterfully on me up against the tiles under the cascading water of the gym's shower. I had thought of the churning of his cock inside me, the strength of his arms around me, and the silkiness of his hair against my skin ever since that threesome.

He was good at his word about showing me how much he valued this meeting. He had booked a room in Bangkok's most exclusive hotel, the Oriental, on the banks of the Chaopya River in the center of the city's commercial area. The first thing I noticed when I was ushered into the eighth-floor room suspended over the busy river was the sumptuous Jim Thompson silk appointments, a model of understated wealth and refinement. The second thing I noticed was the bucket on a table in the center of the room with an uncorked bottle of Mumms champagne cooling in it. I also couldn't miss the tube of lubricant lying next to the champagne bucket alongside a money clip thick with Thai baht, left there no doubt after having tipped the hotel staff heavily in advance to enable this tryst.

The third thing I noticed was the Israeli officer, draped pensively at the corner of the full-length window, dressed in his military khakis and black boots—outfitted Israeli military style at least from the waist down. He was bare chested, those long powerful arms of his folded under his bulging, hair-covered pecs. He had been staring out of the window when I arrived, but as soon as the bellboy departed and quietly clicked the door to the room behind him, the Israeli turned and gave me a broad smile of welcome, obviously delighted that his campaign to meet me again had been successful. He undraped his arms from around his chest and walked over to the table, poured champagne into a glass, and turned to me.

I assumed he was going to hand me the glass of champagne, but he didn't do so right away. Instead, he took a deep drink from the glass himself and then leaned into me. It was obvious he wanted me to kiss him, and when I opened my lips to him, he transferred the champagne into my mouth. He did this twice again before he refilled the glass, handed it to me, and moved to close behind me. He was forceful, almost cocky in his movements. Throughout the preliminaries he was quite precise and authoritative in telling me what he wanted me to do, no doubt, I thought, a natural function of his military position, but also a sign of high self-confidence, as it he assumed I'd acquiesce in anything he asked of me. I might have found his direction brusque and presumptive, but I quickly was finding that I liked this form of domination.

I was wearing a light cotton safari leisure suit from the Bangkok designer, John Fowler, which was popular with the foreign community at that time. The shirt tail was hanging outside my pants, and, moving to behind me, the Israeli ran his hands under that at both of my sides and moved his strong hands up between my shirt and my skin to come resting on my pecs. He pulled my body in close to his front, and I could feel the urgency of his cock against the small of my back. He flicked my nipples and I moaned for him and almost spilled the champagne. One of his hands slid down my belly and followed the thin trail of hair running from my navel down to my pubes. His hand went below my waistband, and he cupped my cock and balls. I groaned and laid my head back against his shoulder, and he kissed my temple.

He started undoing my belt and zipping my pants down, but I put my hand on his and asked him if I could shower first. No one could go out in the noonday sun of Bangkok and avoid getting hot and sticky, and I was no exception in this. He consented, although I could tell he was a little peeved that I had interrupted his own schedule, and waved his hand toward the bathroom. I disengaged from his embrace, placed my obviously very expensive crystal champagne glass carefully down on the table and entered the bath. I was about to shut the door, but he instructed me in a rather gruff voice to leave it open so that he could watch me shower from the bedroom.

I stripped down just inside the bathroom door to give the Israeli a good look at the goods—which, of course weren't really new to him, as he had fully fucked me very recently—and cleaned myself out well with the preparation I'd brought, knowing I had quite an ass session ahead of me. Then, leaving the shower stall open, I took my time washing the grit of the Bangkok streets off my body. When I was finished, I wrapped my body in the lush terrycloth robe the luxury hotel had provided and padded out into the bedroom.

This was the second time I found the Israeli posing pensively against the window overlooking the river, his arms wrapped under his hairy pecs, but this time he was naked. The sun caught and highlighted what was dangling between his legs, and I could have sworn it had grown in length and girth since it had last traveled up my ass.

He turned and smiled at me and beckoned me to the window, where, standing very close in front of me, he slowly untied the sash around my robe, opened it, pulled me to him, and pulled the robe back around us both. I reached for his cock with my hands, but he brushed my hands away, intent on his own campaign.

He kissed me deeply on the lips and his hands were all over my body. He pulled me close, and I felt his cock, insistent, poking at my belly, and his silky pecs were rubbing against mine. After several minutes of this exploration, the Israeli pushed the robe off my back, and turned me and pushed me, rather forcefully, against the full-length window. I was splayed against the window, my palms against the warm glass, and gazed down eight flights to the river below, which was teeming with long-tail boats swamped with fruits and vegetables, as the merchants plied their wares in the water market. The Israeli's mouth was at my ass, and his hands pushed my butt cheeks wide apart to give his tongue and fingers maximum access. He had retrieved the lubricant from the table and worked gobs of that into my asshole with his fingers.

He was driving me wild, and I was sure that he had several fingers fucking up into me as well as his tongue before my legs finally started to give way. I expected him to keep me from collapsing to the thick rug underfoot then and carry me to the bed to make use of my now nicely opened ass canal. But he didn't do that. He supported me with his powerful arms as my knees gave way and I started to sink, but he brought me to the floor on my belly in a controlled collapse. I started to rise, but he barked at me to stay where I was.

One of his arms wound round my belly from behind, and he pulled me up onto my knees on the floor, with my hands palmed on the floor, supporting the weight of my torso. With a loud grunt from him and a low cry of surprise and sharp pain from me, he thrust his hard dick up into me, driving it in to the hilt in one forceful movement, and then he stroked me like this, doggie style, for a good five minutes. I pled with him to slow down, to give me time to adjust to him, but he just laughed and continued stroking hard.

Just when I thought this was going to take him all the way to the finish, he pushed me onto my belly and lay covering me, my legs pulled together between his thighs, and his cock stroking me at an even pace with my canal constricted. His cock was definitely thicker, if not as long, than my Egyptian mentor's, although he was neither as long or as thick as the giant Swede who had taken me in a massage room at the gym a week earlier had been. So, I was doing a good bit of moaning, mouthing off, and writhing under his weight and the power driving of the Israeli's tool, which he seemed to enjoy immensely.

He was definitely the dominating kind, with just a touch of cruelty. If I told him he was fucking me too fast, he'd speed up. If I told him that he was making my nipples sore, he'd dig his fingers deeper into my aureoles and pinch harder. If I told him his hand was crushing my balls, he'd squeeze and pull harder.

A good nearly ten minutes later, he started revolving around his cock inside me until his legs straddled my chest and pushed in, his head was down near my ankles, and his hands were wrapped around my ankles. I felt like a too-thick screw was being twisted down into my too-small hole. I cried out as much in wonder and pleasure at the image of what he was doing to me, though, as in pain.

With the strength of his hip muscles, he then stroked down into my beleaguered canal at a whole new cock angle. Off and on, he wishboned my legs with his hands on my ankles and then brought them back together, giving me a loose and then constricted feel in addition to the different stroke angle. He continued this until he shoot off, me moaning and groaning in new-found appreciation the whole time.

When he was spent and I had felt his cock soften inside me, he, at last, pulled me off of the rug and tossed me onto the bed. He came down beside me, wrapped his strong arms around me, and we both snoozed, I in the warmth and silky softness of his hairy embrace.

Exhausted from the Israeli's calisthenics with and inside my body, I probably could have slept there until evening, but not long after—the sun still streaming in the window, if at a somewhat lower angle that brought its rays up onto the gaily colored smooth silk of the Jim Thompson bedspread—the Israeli woke me with the sensation of intimately search hands around my body once more. A rejuvenated cock was poking at my thigh.

I suggested, still half drowsy, that I was exhausted and sore. He laughed, rose up on his knees, grabbed my hips with his big hands, and roughly pulled me down to where my butt was suspended on the edge of the foot of the bed. He was below me in a flash, holding my legs wide with his hands, and, barely awake, I cried out and arched my back, as he thrust his cock inside me again and rode me hard, his hands cruelly twisting and pinching my nipples and beating my cock, to another ejaculation, with me trying to catch my breath, arching and unarching my back in rhythm with his thrusts, and bunching up the silk bedspread in my fists in an effort to maintain an anchored position.

At length, his rhythm slowed, he brought my legs in to his body so they were propped up against his shoulders, and he started kneading my pecs with his hands, rubbing the nipples, at first gently and then harder again, as he felt himself climaxing— quickening his rhythm again, taking longer, deeper strokes, and throwing his shoulders back as he shot his seed up into me once again out of that thick Israeli canon of his.

He held there for almost a minute, savoring this proof of his virility. Then he patted me on the belly, murmured "good job," and pulled out of me. He padded over to the table supporting the champagne bucket, picked up the money clip, and started pulling off baht bills on the way back to the bed. By the time he got back, me still collapsed, with my butt at the edge of the foot of the bed and my heels dug into the thick carpet, he had pulled off five ten-thousand baht notes (something like $200 at the time). He tossed these down beside me on the bed spread and said, "Great job. Really good with the fresh innocence and mild reluctance act. I'd like to see you again soon, if it can be arranged."

"What?" I exclaimed. It hit me hard, immediately, and right between the eyes. He thought I was an experienced callboy and that the Egyptian was my pimp.

"What?" I repeated, sitting up on the edge of the bed, now all indignant. "You thought I was a male whore? You thought I came here for the money? I didn't. I came here because you attracted me. I didn't give you any sort of an act. You're one of the few men I've been with; I hadn't done this at all before last month. I came here for you, not for your money."

He stood there for the longest minute, stunned at what I was saying. And then he went all red in embarrassment, sank down on his knees in front of me, and apologized profusely between kisses he was applying all over my bruised and roughly fucked body.

In the shower later, as he tenderly soaped and rinsed me off, he apologized again and again for taking me so roughly, saying that he just couldn't control his urge to fuck me and had genuinely thought I sold my body for this sort of sex. Right before he knelt in front of me and serviced my cock, he asked if I could forgive his roughness and meet with him again. I told him that he needn't have worried about that—that I was learning that I wanted to be dominated in just the way he had dominated me.

Chapter Four: Kasem's Kitchen

If the kitchen of Kasem's family in the upcountry jungle of Thailand hadn't burned to the ground, I possibly never would have found out what the special Bangkok sports massage was all about. Kasem was my masseur at a fancy Bangkok gym, which was open for "men only" a couple of nights a week. It was a major pickup place for prime cuts of male meat. Of course, when I'd started going to the gym, I hadn't known it was "that sort of place," and I'd never experienced a male-male coupling before— although I'd certainly given it some serious thought. With my male model and minor TV and movie "the handsome young stud" role background, I apparently qualified as a prime cut, and it wasn't long before I was humping with—and being humped by—the best-endowed of them.

It also wasn't long before I heard about the special Bangkok sports massage that a lot of the guys were getting from their masseurs. But after a couple of months at the gym, with a massage after each workout, my own masseur, Kasem, hadn't shown the least bit of intention of introducing me to any such special massage. I don't want to leave the impression that he didn't give a really good sports massage, though. I never could quite figure out how such a short, thin—almost boyish and shy— Thai man, who I was told was well into his twenties, could have such strong hands and masterful technique. But then, I quickly learned that, with the Thai, looks were deceiving. They could look like they were weak and starving, but they'd show out to be able to manhandle grand pianos up three flights of stairs in a solo effort.

Kasem's family house lost its kitchen to a stove fire, which, fortunately, was set away from the main structure of their house, in keeping with Thai good common sense practices. And to get money to rebuild, the family was forced to come to their "rich" city son—who would be the masseur Kasem (who probably was rich by Thai standards from the tips he made from farang—foreign clients). But Kasem was stretched for money himself, so he passed on his family's plight to his clients.

Kasem didn't hit me directly for financial help when he initially told me of his family's dire problem. But he started softening me up while he told me about the tragedy. I was flat on my belly on the massage table, completely naked, as that's how all massages were given at the gym. Kasem was deep massaging the backs of my thighs, when I felt him pull my thighs apart, and he was massaging the inner thighs right up to the groin.

This was a little farther than he'd ever gone before, and his touch was sending electric shocks through my body. He moved one hand to the small of my back to keep me pressed down on the table and his other, well-oiled hand wrapped itself around my cock, which he had brought back through my legs. And he slowly stroked me to ejaculation, all the time chattering on about how difficult it was to live life in rural Thailand when your kitchen had burned down.

He wasn't drawing attention to the almost surreptitious hand job he was giving me, and I, other than the sighing and moaning I was doing, didn't bring any attention to it either. I was afraid that if what he was doing was openly acknowledged, I would be breaking some sort of unspoken rule, and he'd stop short of giving me satisfaction and release.

But he didn't stop, and it was very nice—a whole new, pleasant sensation for me. It was about as relaxing as a post-gym session massage could get. I left thinking, "So this is what a special Bangkok massage is all about. Very nice; I'm glad I finally found out about that." And I tipped Kasem an extra 50 baht (which was all of about 20 cents U.S. at the time. But that was considered a handsome sum to be tipped on top of the usual 100 baht.)

The next week, I was feeling a little deflated when my massage was about over, because Kasem had already done my back and now had me turned over. If he was going to give me what I thought was a Bangkok special, it should have happened by now. I was panicking. Could it be that I hadn't tipped him enough the previous session? That I had somehow insulted him? But then, while he was massaging my chest and belly, he started talking about that kitchen again and lamenting about the exorbitant estimate the family had been given for reconstruction of this very necessary section of their home. It could come to almost as much as 30,000 baht (only some $115, but more than most rural families could make in a year in combined income).

I suddenly realized that only one hand was massaging my chest and belly now; the other hand was rubbing my inner thighs and eventually worked its way to my engorging cock. I drew in my breath with a hiss as I felt the foreskin of my cock being pulled down to the rim of my glans and an oily finger beginning to massage my mushroom cap, mixing oil with the precum that started to bubble up. Rubbing it around the cock head, a finger was trying to insert itself into my piss slit. I arched my back in sensual pleasure and tried, quite unsuccessfully, not to groan, as Kasem proceeded to rub oil all over my cock and balls and slowly jerked me off. Once again, we both pretended that nothing was happening beyond the usual sports massage.

I tipped Kasem an extra 100 baht and left thinking, Ah, this must be the Bangkok special massage. Much more than all right!

The third week, while I once more was on my back, was when Kasem broached the possibility that I might be able to lend him the 30,000 baht his family needed to build a kitchen. And maybe we could think of some way he could work off the debt in installments. Little doubt was left about what the installments might consist of, because immediately after making the proposal, Kasem swallowed my cock and started deep throating it. I had my hands buried in his thick, wiry black hair and was moaning loud enough to be heard in the next massage cubicle (which was tit for tat, because I had heard enough moaning from the other cubicles during my earlier tame massages). By the time oiled fingers began making little forays into my pulsing asshole, I was ready to give Kasem anything he asked for.

Of course I'd loan him the money to rebuild the family kitchen. I left him with what I had in my wallet, about 5,000 baht, I think, and promised him the balance when I returned to the gym the next week.

He was so delighted the next week, when I handed over a full 30,000 baht and suggested that the family install an extra special new kitchen that, after he had pounded, prodded, and kneaded my body to sheer suppleness, he climbed up on the massage table, straddled my hips between his wiry, strong thighs, and made my throbbing cock disappear up his asshole. He rode my dick for a good thirty minutes, making every pelvis movement imaginable and dispensing love to every square inch of my buried cock. I was letting him know of my pleasure so loudly and graphically that I'm sure that everyone in the surrounding cubicles was envious and made sure he had special massages of his own that evening.

On the fifth week, Kasem wanted to start talking about a repayment schedule. He seemed to think it would take six months or more to pay me off, but I suggested a way of making the schedule much, much shorter. The first installment of my idea of a schedule had Kasem kneeling in a side chair with his belly draped over the chair back and me standing behind him, holding his pert little hips in my hands, and fucking my hot and ready cock up into his hole until the loud groans and moans those in the other cubicles were enjoying were coming out in a throaty, high-pitched Thai rather than English.

I never did learn, in terms of sexual services rendered, where a regular Bangkok special sports massage stopped and fulfillment of a loan repayment plan began. But Kasem must have thought the arrangement was a good one, because when I left Bangkok for a new assignment in Japan, he came to the airport to see my family off. And, with tears in his eyes, he thanked me for helping his family rebuild their kitchen. My wife was very touched, both that my masseur would make a special trip to bid me farewell and that I was so philanthropic.

Chapter Five: The Cast Party

I could not have been in any steamier place or time for my sexual awakening. Bangkok, Thailand, in the eighties was sin city extraordinaire. Anything went there; everything was tolerated. It was a mai bin rai ("nevermind; whatever, it's OK") place, and everything was not only tolerated, but it also was on offer—and almost always for free or at a very good price. And, in some regards, it was a sexually innocent time. The mellow follow-on years after the hippy era of "if it feels good, do it" and before anyone had ever heard the term AIDS.

The U.S. government was also partly to blame for my development of an interest in the gay life style. I was a young government pilot of the SR71 photo-reconnaissance aircraft, and politics had shut us down for several months of my Bangkok tour. This had allowed me to turn my interests elsewhere other than soaring higher above the earth than anyone else could at the time.

I had time on my hands, and, thus, when there was a casting call for the Bangkok Community Theatre's production of the new Ira Leven thriller Deathtrap, to be performed at the Bhirasri Institute off Sathorn Road, I auditioned and won the part of the young protagonist, Clifford Anderson. I had acted through high school and college, including as background sand stud in beach movies, and exotic Bangkok had set my creative juices boiling. Opposite me, in the older man's role of Sidney Bruhl, was an expatriate queen in his late forties who I will call Ron (primarily because that was his name).

Ron had taught English for years at the American University Association in Bangkok. He was banished from the United States by his rich family because he had the gall to be gay at a time when it wasn't fashionable—at least flamboyantly and in public. He had outlived his family, however, and had inherited their money. So he was having the last laugh by living in style in a mansion near Sathorn Road with his choice of young men who were interested in his money (and in each other).

Ron had been attracted to me, and he regularly gave me expert, soft-mouthed blowjobs in our shared dressing room throughout the run of the play to release the tension we both felt after an exhilarating performance. I also fucked him doggy style once at his request, but I'll have to admit that I found his blowjobs more satisfying. He asked me to move into the mansion with him and his friends then, but I didn't consider myself for sale—driving a stealth jet paid quite well—and not to mention that I had a wife and children and an entirely different life I wasn't going to abandon.

At the time, Ben, a U.S. Army lieutenant assigned to the Joint U.S. Military Advisory Group was living with Ron, and Ben threw Ron a cast party at the mansion following the closing night of the play.

All of the women and straight men involved in the play departed the party early, no doubt not all that comfortable with the special friends Ben had invited to Ron's party. But I stayed on.

I had realized by this time that this was a special time and place for me, sexually, and I wanted to make the most of it. It wasn't long before my wish was granted.

I was returning from the bathroom, half snookered, down a long, dark hallway, when I was accosted by Ron's live-in, Ben. He just turned my back to the wall in the hallway, planted his palms on either side of my shoulders, and came in for a long, wet kiss. Ben was pretty much a hunk, so I just went with the flow. It was a hot evening, and everyone left was starting to shed clothes. I had my shirt open and Ben had no shirt on at all. He rubbed his chest and basket against mine and made me feel pretty rubbery in the knees.

After another kiss on the lips and a couple on my nipples, he told me to turn around, belly to the wall, and I did so. He took my shirt off me and then stripped down my pants and briefs, so that all I was wearing were my loafers. He placed his hands on my hips where they joined my waist, with his thumbs across my butt cheeks, and I remember thinking that this simple gesture seemed to mark his full possession of me, at least for that moment. If I'd ever had the inclination to cut and run, this ended any such thought. He kissed and tongued his way down my back. He knelt behind me and must have taken his own pants off then, because I wasn't aware of that happening later, and I felt a hand come between my thighs and signal that I was supposed to open up my stance, which I did. The hand came on through and pulled my cock back between my legs and stroked it, while his tongue and lips searched for—and found—my asshole in the folds of my butt cheeks. All the while, the music and laughter were wafting down the hall at us from the living areas of the mansion.

I had my hands raised to either side of my shoulders and my palms and cheek hugged the cool plaster interior wall of the old mansion. I wasn't thinking anything except what a new exhilarating experience I was having. All of my senses were focused on the cock and the asshole that this handsome hunk of an army lieutenant were making love to. I was footloose in Bangkok, my family having gone back to the states early for summer R&R. Everything was allowed as long as it felt good. And this felt great.

Ben was alternating the attention his mouth was giving me between tonguing and rimming my asshole and sucking and twirling his tongue around the tender bulb of my cock. He was moistening up my asshole really good, but my cock was getting too stiff to hold the between-the-legs angle, so Ben told me to turn around, and he sucked me off from the front. His right hand was running over my thighs and my belly up to my chest, and he was using his left hand to either work my balls or gently finger fuck my ass.

Meanwhile, there were men going back and forth down the hallway to use the bathroom. One beautiful blond Scandinavian showed particular interest in what we were doing and came back to observe briefly at various intervals of this fantastic experience I was having. But most took what we were doing for granted—they all were doing similar things all over the house that evening themselves. Ben was one of the best-looking, and certainly one of the best hung, men at the party. And I was vain enough to be quite assured of my own qualities in both regards as well, so I wasn't at all embarrassed at giving anyone a show who wanted one. What I lacked in experience at that point I made up for in enthusiasm and the willingness to shed all inhibitions.

After I had come at the back of Ben's throat, he stood back up and kissed me on the lips for a few more moments. Then he sort of stooped down in front of me, braced his arms under my butt, and told me to help lift myself and climb up on his waist. He was very strong and I didn't have to help him raise me up much at all. I hooked my legs above his hips and wrapped my arms around his chest below his armpits. I immediately felt his cock head at my asshole.

He entered me a couple of inches and waited for me to adjust to him. He had two strong hands under my thighs. Then he slowly slid a long, slender cock up my ass canal. It felt almost like I was taking in an eel. I figured he must have been a good eight or nine inches long, but he wasn't all that thick. And then, for a good long time he just fucked me against that wall, using his strong leg muscles and those hands under my thighs to move me. He held his cock steady deep inside me and worked my pelvis up and down for the stroking and pumping action. I moved my arms up around his neck and buried my face in the hollow of his neck and savored the fuck—enjoying his hard, strong body. I absorbed the feeling of his chest and belly heaving and rubbing up and down mine almost as much as I enjoyed the feeling of him slithering around inside me.

After he had jacked off in me, he let my feet back down on the floor and gave me another wet and deep kiss on the mouth. He told me how nice I was and that he'd wanted to do that the entire time the play was rehearsing and that he'd planned this party just so he and I could hook up. Then he said he had other guests to contend with, so he'd have to leave me, but that he hoped we could be special friends in the future. (As it turned out, we became very special, close friends in various parts of the world thereafter.)

I was told later that the aging queen, Ron, had seen me together with his live-in in that hallway and had retreated to his room in tears. I don't know if that was the case, but he avoided me thereafter for the rest of my tour in Bangkok. I sort of regretted the loss of that very experienced soft mouth of his.

I returned to the party to find that it had become quite raucous. Many of the guests had wound up nude in the pool, and I joined them there. This certainly was a good way to shop what was available in Bangkok and who had the longest and thickest goods and the best build. I was happy to see that in that time of my life I measured up very well to the competition.

I found the blond Scandinavian voyeur from earlier in the evening sitting on the side of the pool dangling his legs—and very nearly his horse-hung dong as well, I might add—in the water, and I swam up to him and sucked his dick until it was hard and was standing at attention. He enjoyed that so much that he hauled me up out of the pool, and almost literally carried me over to a nearby lounge and side-split fucked me for three-quarters of an hour or more. I'll never forget what wonders he could do with a nipple while he was plowing my ass deep and stretching my canal walls to the limit. I was late in learning that the nipple was an erogenous zone for many a man—and most certainly for me. I have large aureoles around my nipples and get sent over the moon any time a man takes all of that in his mouth and gives it suck. I think that alone can add an extra inch and a half to my hardened cock. All of these "first discoveries" thrilled me.

While I was being plowed by the Scandinavian, I chanced to look over to a nearby pool lounge and saw the man of my dreams, a hulky chocolate brown hunk with the biggest, thickest cock I had ever seen until then—and since then as far as I can remember. He was fascinating to watch as he hunched over a reclining blond and pistoned down into his ass—not the least because his attention-commanding cock was several shades darker than he was. He looked at me and smiled for me and I knew right there and then that I would be going after him in the weeks to come. I was later to know him simply as the major.

Bangkok in the early eighties was perfect for sexual awakenings. Nothing was taboo. Everything was done for the sheer pleasure of it.

Chapter Six: Ten Slash Two

I had been jittery and conflicted for the entire two weeks since I'd seen that big black topping a guy at a pool party in Bangkok. I had been bottoming for a Swede in a nearby patio lounge when I looked over and saw this monster cock jackhammering in out of the other guy—who clearly was in seventh heaven—and I almost melted on the spot. I was in conflict, though. Obsessed with desire because the cock, even more distinctive because it was almost jet black and was attached to a bulky—but ripped bulky—milk-chocolate body, looked so desirable. But threatened because the sheer size of it filled me with fear and uncertainty. I'd only been doing this for a short time. Was it even possible to take something like that in?

I couldn't get it out of mind, and a couple of days later I had the opportunity to ask the host of the party, Ben, who the guy was.

"Ah, we call him 10/2," was the answer. "He's an army major at JUSMAG. Luscious, isn't he?"

"10/2?" I asked, somewhat bewildered.

"Yeah," the host said, with a little snicker. "That's like in inches, both ways."

"Oh."

"Yes, oh. Biggest combined stats we have in service here, as far as I know. Interested?" the host asked, not showing the least amount of jealously, even though he had fucked me at the party himself—and must have enjoyed that, because he had just finished fucking me again on the rattan-carpeted teak floor of his Bangkok mansion when I asked him this question.

"Just curious," I said, nibbling at one of my host's nipples to give him reassurances. "But I think I'll refer to him as 'the major.' Less shocking."

"Well, if it's more than curiosity, forget going after him," Ben replied. "He does the picking. If he wants you, you'll get an invitation."

I don't know if Ben had passed on my interest or if the big black had seen me at that pool party and liked what he saw, but not long after that I got the invitation.

Although I wasn't military, my SR71 supersonic jet unit was under military cover, and so I usually fell in with whatever the U.S. military establishment in Thailand had going. Thus, only about a week after that, I was invited to a change of command ceremony for the chief of JUSMAG, the Joint U.S. Military Assistance Group in Thailand. The speeches were still droning on, with all of us standing, if not exactly at attention, when I felt this big hand cup one of my butt cheeks. I didn't dare look around, and it could have been one of several guys I had been meeting at Ben's Bangkok mansion. In fact, I had assumed it was Ben, because he was a JUSMAG lieutenant himself, and I knew he was attending this ceremony. But, the voice that whispered in my ear in a deep melodious tone clearly was not Ben's.

"I've heard you've been asking about me." the voice whispered.

I turned and looked up, which was humble in itself, because I wasn't short, and found myself staring into the glittering eyes of the major—the one others called 10/2. I felt overwhelmed by his muscled bulk as he stood very close behind me. I was speechless. The hand on my butt cheek applied pressure, as he continued.

"I saw you at the party at Ben's a couple of weeks ago."

A weak and breathy "Oh" was all I could manage to squeak out. There would be no fooling him, then.

"I'd like to have you for lunch today . . . at my place . . . unless you have other plans. My car's here. I could drop you back here if you've driven or take you home after . . . lunch . . . if you don't have wheels."

What could I say—assuming that I could catch my breath to say anything at all, that is. I just nodded dumbly, wearing, I'm sure, the sloppiest of grins.

By the time we'd reached his Thai-style elevated teak house, hidden in a lush tropical garden beside a klong, one of those waterways lacing through the city that made Bangkok the Venice of the East, I was trembling all over from fear and anticipation and could hardly make my way from the car and up the stairs into his nearly wall-less platform house under my own steam.

There was, of course, no lunch waiting for us, and, indeed, I had not had any illusions what was going to be fed into me on this excursion. The black army major motioned with one hand, sending servants scurrying for the stairway and out to the corners of the compound, I'm sure, to afford us total privacy, while he guided me straight to his bedroom with the other hand.

Centered in this room was a gigantic, mosquito net-draped four-poster bed, set on a teak-board floor. The three exterior walls were actually wooden louvered folding doors running between circular tree-trunk columns. The doors could be shut at night for privacy, but they were all open now, and the foliage of the deep green jungle trees, laced with wild orchids, pressed in at us from all three exterior sides. A ceiling fan revolved lazily overhead. The air was heavy with humidity. I felt the jungle closing in on me, and I was immobilized by trepidation. I couldn't get that ten-inch long, two-inch thick ebony cock out of my mind.

And very soon thereafter, it no longer was in my mind, but was there before me. I stood dumbly beside the bed, as the big black stripped my clothes off me and placed them neatly on a side chair. He held me at arms' length, and then drew me to him and kissed me deeply on the mouth. He let me virtually fall into a sitting position on the end of the bed, as my knees gave out and then he stood and stripped before me, revealing that monster that soon would be splitting me asunder.

He came to me, pushing me down on my back on the bed, opening my legs with knees that knelt on the edge of the bed, taking my wrists in his big hands and spreading my arms wide across the bedspread. He then dipped his head, first down to mine for searching kisses on the lips, and then traveled his lips down to my nipples. After an eternity of attention here, he followed the thin trail of hair from my pecs down and around my navel and into my pubic region, his knees now down on the floor and his barrel chest between my spread legs.

I was sighing and moaning and giving little mewing sounds—and quite frankly was beginning to hyperventilate, my mind obsessed with what he was packing between his legs—both longer and thicker than anything I'd attempted thus far.

His lips, tongue, and teeth were at the rim of my asshole and then invading me, loosening me up—or at least trying to. I think that, rather, I was tightening up the longer I thought of his equipment and what it might do to me.

He obviously felt me tighten up, because he stood up then, between my legs, giving quite a good view of his now-hardened cock, the sight of which, of course, wasn't helping dispel my gathering fear.

"What's wrong?" he asked. "You are tightening. Don't you want it?"

"Yes, of course, I want it, but I'm afraid of your size. Can't you feel me trembling?"

"Ah," he said. "I saw you with the Swede. I'm just a bit longer and thicker than he was. I'm sure you can take me. But, I'll tell you what. Unless you want to just stop—and you'll trust me—we can try something that's worked on others. Do you want to try?"

"Yes," I answered in a tiny voice. I was dying to take that cock. I'd try anything that might work.

"Have you fucked with mild bondage?" He asked.

"Once or twice," I admitted.

"And how did that make you feel? Did you tense up more or did you relax, no longer having the responsibility for what was happening?"

"I guess I relaxed at bit," I admitted.

In no time at all, I was on my chest on the bed, my wrists loosely tied with leather strips to the slats of the headboard, up on my knees, and with my butt in the air. The big black worked my ass at length with his tongue and lips, with a lubricant, and, eventually with an increasing number of fingers.

No longer having any responsibility at all, I did find myself loosening to his attention, which included hands flowing all over my body, exploring all of my curves and crevices, making intimate love to me.

The finger fucking became progressively more painful as more fingers were added and they went deeper, until a certain peak was achieved and then the pleasure flooded in. The fingers probed deeper and deeper, and I widened my stance as much as I could, trying mightily to take them all in. Deeper, deeper. Impossibly deeper.

"I had no idea your fingers were so long and thick," I managed to speak between moans and pants.

"Those aren't fingers, Sport." the major whispered with a little laugh. "I've been cocking you for several minutes now. I'm in. And now that you know I'm in, I'll run it to the end and start stroking you. You're doing fine. You've got a sweet ass. You're doing fine."

He stroked me and stroked me and stroked me, until he came deep inside me, and then he stayed in me, still filling me to the limit as he became tumescent, and reached under and stroked my cock until I came. We lay, his beefy black body covering mine, my knees now collapsed and my body stretched out under his on the top of the bed, as we both recovered, reloaded, rearroused.

Then he released my imprisoned hands, turned me over on my back, and pulled me back to the foot of the bed.

The fear was over. I had accommodated him, and I had loved being fucked by him. I now couldn't get enough of his ripped body and that vigorous ten- by two-inch muscle at his center. He was standing on the floor between my widespread legs now, hunched a bit over me, his gigantic manhood and huge balls swaying below his flat belly. My heart was racing and I was moaning, overcome with anticipation, as his milk chocolate, beefy-fingered hands glided over the creamy white skin of my thighs, belly, and chest. I groaned as rough-padded fingers rubbed, and twitched, and pinched my tender nipples.

I arched my chest up from bed, wanting to see as much of his stud-muscled body as I could as he worked my arousal zones. I cried out as his full lips found my nipples and his mouth opened around my aureoles, closed tight, and gave suck. I melted to his teeth sliding across my engorged nipples. I opened my mouth wide to gasp at the hint of a bite on a nipple, only to have his heavy lips crush mine, and his thick tongue push in. I opened my eyes to his, very close now, filled with desire, determination, insistence.

As I eased my back down on the bed, he rose up below me. Breathlessly, I watched giant hands gliding across my body, slowly working their way to my center. Milk chocolate hands on soft, creamy white belly and thighs, nudging. Mesmerized, I opened my legs to him. Purring sounds involuntarily escaped my lips as hands glided around silky inner thighs.

The body of the hulking black army officer sank toward the floor between my opened legs, and his grinning face dipped out of sight. I arched my back and gasped again, as his thick tongue once again rimmed, flicked in, and then invaded my ass canal. Grasping the close-cropped kinky black hair of the head bobbing at my crotch, my immediate impulse was to push the invader away, but this was quickly replaced with desire to hold the swaying orb in closer to my center. I began twitching and trembling to the dancing of the tongue, but this no longer was a sign of fear and dreaded anticipation, but of ecstasy.

Big, thick fingers snaked in, thicker than some men's cocks, exploring, searching. An agony of mixed pain, pleasure, and expectation flooded me in the brief seconds it took him to center. I writhed against his possessing hand as it found the prostate, tweaking it, rubbing it, and quickening the flow of precum from my aching cock.

I panted and moaned for him and shouted my burning desire and pleasure to the giant rustling leaves of jungle trees pressing in on us beyond the teak columns. A bolt of electricity rushed through my body and sparks flew, as my cock's trigger snapped and my cum flew.

I heard a low, satisfied, hoarse laugh from between my trembling legs.

The muscle-bound milk chocolate army officer, with his jet-black 10/2 monster cock and plump balls stood in possessing triumph between my spread legs now. His massive chest and arm muscles bulged and undulated, glistening in the heavy atmosphere and the strobing of light through the waving leaves and the languidly moving blades of the overhead fan. A big grin on his square-cut face, he captured and placed my hands so I could feel the awesome length and thickness (and the bulbous, purple-black cap and popped-out blue-on-black veins) of his hardened cock. My fearful fingers trembled at the measure of the beast, all the more imposing in its blackness against his otherwise milk chocolate, while he told me quite clearly and graphically—and breathtakingly—what he was going to do with all that manhood and how much pleasure he was getting—and expected to continue to get—out of me and expected me still to get out of his cock—to the point of making me tremble in anticipation. He told me that I never again, with any other man, would be fucked this completely and fulfilled to this extent—and he was right. Never again with others, but always with him. I suspected, even then, that he would be right, because I could not imagine any higher ecstasy that he now was giving me.

I went up on my elbows, my legs splayed up and out, my ankles held in his big hands, and watched him first, slap that monster cock against my butt cheeks, and then rub it up and down and around there. He then stroked it up and down in my crack, across my puckered asshole, teasing me, dry fucking me, driving me wild, making me beg for him to ram it back inside me. He rotated that purple-black cap around and just inside the rim, entirely with the control he had over his hips and his hardened cock—no help with his hands. And then slowly, almost magically, he made the pillar of power and strength follow its bulbous head and disappear inside me, me arching my back, trying to stretch to accommodate him and involuntarily giving him deep moans and groans of being stuffed.

"No, no; yes, yes, y-e-s. It's too big; it's the size I've always dreamed of. It's splitting me; it's stretching and filling me to perfection. I can't take this; I can't get enough of this. Yesssssss!"

Bringing his mouth down to my nipples as he plowed me, he sucked and bit me lightly there.

I felt the veins of his thick pole sliding against my ass walls as his cock journeyed in to the quick. Then he rose back on the balls of his feet again, hunched over me, and repeatedly pulled his glistening jet-black cock out slowly to where I could again see the rim of the purple-black cap, and then glided it back in to the root until he eventually lost control in his own trip to Nirvana and started pumping me wildly (showing that he panted for me as much as I did for him). At the height of his passion, he dipped his mouth to mine and brutalized my lips with his. His hands grabbed my hips and moved my pelvis in and out, up and down, revolving around to meet and enhance his thrusts. He cried out. Again he was flooding the inside me with fountains of cum, so strong and full that it oozed out of me and bathed those black balls of his.

All of that was still throbbing inside me, hard for me, wanting to be inside me, and filling me repeatedly—followed by my insides being creamed again and again with his semen and him holding for a few minutes, young, virile, powerful, quick loading. And then doing it all again. And my being able to take it, each time more slippery than the last because of the accumulation and mingling of juices—and then he turned me on his cock until he was close in behind me, capable of going even deeper inside me, and then fucking me again, holding my wrists with his hands, dominating me. Him shooting off every fifteen minutes or so for what seems like forever—me climaxing repeatedly, encasing that jet-black 10/2 hunk and being encased by that milk chocolate rippling network of perfect muscle.

The fuck of my life.

Chapter Seven: Power of the Major Emphasized

Heart racing, moaning, shimmering with anticipation, as milk chocolate, beefy-fingered hands glide over creamy white skin. Trembling as they search for and explore curves and crevices, zeroing in on heaving breasts. Groaning as rough-padded fingers rub, and twitch, and pinch tender nipples. Arching chest up from bed before the hovering milk chocolate monolith, rising to the inevitable. Crying out as full lips find nipples and mouth opens around aureoles, closes tight, and gives suck. Melting at teeth sliding across engorged nipples. Opening mouth to gasp at the hint of a bite on a nipple, only to have heavy lips crush mine and thick tongue push in. Opening eyes to his, very close now, filled with desire, determination, insistence.

Easing back on bed, as he rises up below me. Breathless as I watch giant hands gliding across my body, slowly working their way to my center. Milk chocolate hands on soft, creamy white belly and thighs, nudging. Mesmerized, I open my legs to him. Purring as hands glide around silky inner thighs.

Hulking soldier sinks between opened legs, grinning face dipping out of sight. Arching back and gasping again, as thick tongue rims, flicks in, and then invades. Grasping close-cropped kinky black hair, immediate impulse to push away, quickly replaced with desire to hold in closer. Twitching to the dancing of the tongue. Big, thick finger snaking in, thicker than some men's cocks, exploring, searching. Agony in the brief seconds found to center. Writhing as it finds the spot, tweaks, rubs, and quickens the flow. Panting, moaning. Can't . . . get . . . breath. Electricity, sparks, release and flow. Low, hoarse laughter from between trembling legs.

Muscle-bound milk chocolate soldier, with his jet-black monster cock and plump balls, standing between spread legs, his massive chest and arm muscles bulging and undulating, glistening in the strobing of light through the languidly moving blades of the overhead fan. A big grin on his square-cut face, capturing and placing my hands so I feel the awesome length and thickness (and the bulbous, purple-black cap and popped-out blue-on-black veins) of his hardened cock. Fearful fingers getting the measure of the beast, all the more imposing in its blackness against his otherwise milk chocolate, while he tells me quite clearly and graphically—and breathtakingly—what he is going to do with all that manhood and how much pleasure he is going to get out of me and expects me to get out of his cock—to the point of making me tremble in anticipation (and having the added pleasure that, out of all those he could pick to fuck this day, he is here with me).

Going up on my elbows, my legs splayed up and out, my ankles held in his big hands, and watching him first rotate that purple-black cap around and just inside the rim, entirely with the control he has over his hips and his hardened cock—no help with his hands. And then slowly, almost magically, making the pillar of power and strengthen follow its bulbous head and disappear inside me, me arching my back, trying to stretch to accommodate him and involuntarily giving him deep moans and groans of being stuffed. No, no; yes, yes, y-e-s. It's too big; it's the size I've always dreamed of. It's splitting me; it's stretching and filling me to perfection. I can't take this; I can't get enough of this. Yesssssss!

Bringing his mouth down to my nipples as he plows me, sucking and biting me there. My imagining I can feel the veins sliding against my ass walls as the cock journeys in to the quick, and then him standing up from me and repeatedly pulling his glistening jet-black cock out slowly to where I can again see the rim of the purple-black cap, and glide it back in to the root until he loses control and starts pumping me wildly (showing that he is panting for me—at the height of his passion, dipping his mouth to mine and brutalizing my lips with his). His hands grabbing my hips, moving my pelvis with his thrusts. He cries out. Again the flood inside me, oozing out of me, bathing those black balls.

All of that throbbing inside me, hard for me, wanting to be inside me, and filling me repeatedly—followed by my insides being creamed yet again with his semen and him holding for a few minutes, young, virile, powerful, quick loading. and then doing it all again. And my being able to take it, each time more slippery than the last because of the accumulation and mingling of juices— and then turning me on his cock until he is close in behind me, capable of going even deeper inside me, and then fucking me again, holding my wrists with his hands, dominating me. Him shooting off every fifteen minutes or so for what seems like forever—me climaxing repeatedly, encasing that jet-black hunk of licorice and being encased by that milk chocolate rippling network of perfect muscle.

My ten-by-two major, having me whenever, wherever, however he wants me, whenever he beckons.

Chapter Eight: The Golden Triangle

I hadn't been at my new—and first—embassy posting for more than three days when the Vientiane chief of station called me into his office to give me an important assignment.

"Yes, I can see how important the assignment is, Luther," I said to the Agency's head spy in Laos, "But why me? I mean I didn't finish training at the Farm until three weeks ago, and I'm barely on the ground here and you're already giving me a make or break assignment."

"Look around, Win," Luther said in a slow drawl, as the paddle fan flapped overhead trying to coax out a breeze in the humid afternoon. "Do you see a whole lot of American agents just sitting around here waiting for an assignment? Besides, you fit the bill precisely for what we need."

I didn't know exactly what Luther meant by that comment. The Agency wanted to infiltrate a team into China's Yunnan Province, and Vientiane station was assigned the job of negotiating with the Kwei Lin, the Mien tribe warlord of the Miang Sing area of Laos bordering on China and Myanmar for passage through his region and guides across the Chinese border. The Agency was prepared to overlook Kwei Lin's opium operations through Thailand, since there wasn't a whole heck of a lot that the United States or anyone else could do to stem the flow of heroin from the Golden Triangle anyway, in exchange for Kwei

Lin's help. But why, I wondered, did I fit the bill for the assignment—other than being the only one available, I concluded.

"We have a sweetener for Kwei Lin," Luther was telling me in explanation. "He has a weakness for *farang*—that means Westerners here—blondes, and we're sending a bit of honey with you for him to gaze at during the negotiations and then to have overnight as a reward for giving us favorable terms. Her name's Gail, which is all even you need to know about her. And you are a big, young, strapping dude, so I figure you can get her up north in good condition for Kwei."

I met Gail for the first time on the tarmac before boarding the small plane that would take us up to Chiang Rai, Thailand, where we'd pick up a Mien escort back across the Mekong River and into northwest Laos to meet with Kwei Lin at Miang Sing. Gail was a gorgeous Nordic blonde with melon breasts straining at the fabric of her cotton jungle shirt, which was unbuttoned down to where she was showing a cavern of cleavage that made my groin boil.

We were sitting knees to knees, facing each other, on the two-hour flight in the small plane, and I spent the whole time slowly insinuating my knees between hers and planning how I was going to get my hands on that mound of flesh between her cotton-pants-clad thighs. All the time she was teasing me, acting like she didn't even know I was there, but I could tell that she was interested as well, because of the looks she gave me when she didn't think I was noticing and the hardness of her nipples against the flimsy cotton shirt.

I had my hands on her knees and was working my way toward paradise, when Gail covered my hands with hers.

"I don't think that's really a good idea, Win," she said. "You are here to protect me from this. Maybe afterward . . . and maybe not," she added to tantalize me.

"I think you want this as much as I do," I said in a lust-clogged husky voice.

"Be that as it may," she answered primly. "We have an important job to do here. Or am I the only one here willing to make such a sacrifice for the Agency?"

I couldn't argue with that.

We landed in Chiang Rai near twilight and were hustled off immediately to a dinner in an open-air fish restaurant alongside a water lily-clogged *klong* waterway. Gail looked ravishing in the light from the torches reflecting in the water, and I wanted to rip her clothes off and fuck her right there. She allowed me to run my fingers up and down the soft, blonde down on her forearms, but when one of my hands went to her knee under the table, she laughed and slapped at it.

She rose and went to the ladies' room in a separate hut back in the shadows of the restaurant. I followed her and when she came out of the ladies' room, I pulled her around the corner of the hut on a wooden porch suspended over the klong and pushed her up against the hut wall with my body. She started to object, but I covered her mouth in a brutal kiss that took her breath away. I cupped one of her breasts with a hand and got a hard nipple between two fingers. And I went straight for her mound with my other hand. It was warm, and I could feel that it was moist through the cotton pants.

Gail returned the passion of my kiss briefly, her body trembling under my searching hands. But she abruptly stiffened and pushed me away from her and hurried back through the dimly lit restaurant to our table. When I returned, she was telling our escort that she was ready to go to the hotel and wanted to get a full night's sleep before our trip north through the jungle the next day.

I got the cold shoulder all the way to the Suanthip Vana, an exclusive resort with individual guest houses on the outskirts of the city, where we had been booked for the night. Upon arrival at the hotel, Gail and I were whisked off in different directions, our escort having sensed the tension between us and, not knowing what it might be based in, feeling it best to keep us apart. The wrath of the Vientiane station chief was no doubt something our escort didn't want to risk.

I was still very much hot and bothered, and very hard from the brief encounter with Gail at the restaurant, when I was shown into my guest quarters. A massive four poster bed occupied the center of a room that was sensuously decorated in orangish-red Thai silks, and it didn't cool me off to consider what I'd like to be doing with Gail in that bed just now.

Two Thai attendants, one female and one male, both looking very presentable and decked out in matching Thai silk sarongs, were standing at attention by separate posters at the foot of the bed. As I entered the room, the male attendant helped me off with my coat, as the female attendant quizzed me in silky, demur tones whether either of them could do anything to make my stay any more enjoyable or restful. Anything at all she kept saying with a sweet smile on her lips. If I hadn't been so worked up over Gail, I probably wouldn't have been so bold, but in the heat of the moment, I reached over and undid the sash holding up the young woman's sarong, and it fell down around her sandals.

She was no voluptuous Gail, but she was exquisite. Her golden skin shimmered in the soft lighting of the room, and her long, black hair hung down straight to her waist. She was small and thin, with pert little breasts, and was perfectly formed.

The male attendant drew a bath while the woman slowly undressed me.

"Do you do this for all of your guests?" I asked.

"If they want," she answered. But then she went on. "But we offer special treatment to yellow hairs like you. Yellow hair is considered very lucky here in Thailand."

Moments later I was luxuriating in a large tub of warm water. I was laying back against the curve of the tub's side, with my eyes closed. The male attendant was behind me, massaging my shoulders, neck, and temples and helping to ease all of the pent-up tension over Gail from my body, while the female attendant was more than doing her part toward this end. She was in the tub with me, naked, and was straddling my hips with her legs. At first she glided over my skin with a soapy sponge and perfumed water with one hand, as she slowly worked my cock with the other one, stroking me and making me large. I sighed as she then placed the head of my engorged cock at the opening to her cunt. She used my cock to tease out her clit from its folds and rubbed it against her clit until we were both trembling. Then, as the male attendant's massaging of my shoulders and neck muscles worked deeper, the female attendant descended her hips onto my cock and pulled me ever deeper into her and started to slowly pump me with her pelvis.

Before I climaxed, they had me out of the tub, dried off in intimate pattings with deep-pile cotton towels and had me face down on the four-poster bed. The female attendant was crouched above my head and was deeply massaging my back muscles down to my waist, and the male attendant was crouched below me and massaging my legs and my butt cheeks.

I felt that I was drifting off toward sleep, when they rolled me over and the female attendant moved her body over mine, her bottom and vagina to my flicking tongue, and her tongue and soft mouth to my cock. Her luxurious, straight black hair was swishing across my chest, belly, and sides, and I reached up and played with the large, hard nipples of her pert little breasts. I tensed as I sensed that there was more than one mouth and one pair of hands working on my cock and balls and stroking my inner thighs, but the female attendant pulled away long enough to tell me that servicing a yellow hair was a high honor for Thai men as well, and that I would be doing both of them a good turn by allowing they both to make love to me.

It was as if I was drugged with lust and a languidness from the bath, massaging, and other attentions and transported to a world of *mai pen rai*, that convenient Thai world of "never mind" and "taking pleasure openly and guiltlessly where it could be found." The female attendant came up on her knees over my head, giving me easy access to her clit and her sweet, perfumed cunt with my lips and tongue, while I felt that male attendant lower his hips onto mine, facing her. I sensed that they were embracing and kissing above my chest, as his ass channel slowly descended on my still-hard cock. I could feel him trembling with pleasure as my cock made its long journey up his ass canal. And when I was in to the hilt, he slowly started to pump me in short and then longer strokes, until I came deep inside him.

They doused the lights then and were entwined with me in the bed, me facing the female attendant, and the male attendant encasing me from behind, his half-hard cock rubbing against the small of my back. I dozed then until I was brought back to a level of sexual arousal by four hands gliding across the curves and crevices of my body. I rolled over on top of the female attendant and rubbed and explored her cunt and clit with the fingers of one of my hands until her juices were flowing and she was writhing under me. I fucked her then, hard and fast and deep, while the male attendant crouched behind me and massaged my butt cheeks and thighs.

I fell wearily back into the double embrace of my attendants and went into a deep sleep. When I awoke later, shortly before dawn, to the sound of a brief torrent of rain pelting the thatched roof of the guesthouse, I was alone. I drifted off to sleep again and awoke to the smell of strong coffee coming from a breakfast tray set out on a coffee table in front of a small sofa and perfumed smells from the bathroom. A bath had been drawn for me, and the water was still warm. When I returned to the room, my clothes had been laid out on a made bed. But my attendants from the night before, or their replacements, were nowhere to be seen.

Gail was still acting decidedly cool toward me as we started out north in the morning in a couple of jeeps. She made sure we were in separate vehicles. She'd dolled herself up for the encounter with Kwei Lin in a three-quarter-length cotton skirt and matching halter top in a sky blue that set off her blonde complexion to perfection. But I had no delusions that she'd be looking nearly this fresh when we reached Kwei Lin's mountain stronghold at Miang Sing.

We crossed the Mekong into Laos, near the Myanmar border at Mae Sai, and it was here that I learned both just how well Gail had prepared for Kwei Lin and that she wasn't nearly as cool toward me as she wanted me to think. The Mekong was in full flow, and our primitive wooden barge nearly capsized. We were drenched with brown water, and Gail clutched at me in fear as we were nearly swept away. I held on to her for dear life, not being all that brave or assured myself, and the cotton of her skirt and halter top went transparent, revealing that she was wearing nothing under them.

While our escort and the boatmen fought the river for control of the barge, I was getting a very good feel of both a very nice set of tits and of Gail's pussy through the thin, wet material. She wasn't fighting me either. Our mouths latched in a searching kiss, but we abandoned that almost immediately and tried to put some distance between ourselves when the boat started to win over the current and our escorts were able to parcel out their attention to more than just keeping us alive.

We rode in the back of an ancient truck from the border up into the mountain jungle of northwestern Laos. As we were jostled back and forth, we dried off slowly in the humid air. Gail and I purposely sat across from each other in the truck bed, drinking each other in with our eyes for the remainder of the trip. At one point, the two tribesmen who were assuring us a safe escort into the Mien warlord's fiefdom were jabbering and pointing to Gail and me in an animated fashion. When I asked our interpreter what they were saying, he reiterated what I had heard the night before about yellow-haired farangs being good luck and how rare it was to see two more yellow hairs together in this region—that Gail and I could be taken as twins. I meant to ask the interpreter what they meant by "more yellow hairs" in this remote area, but I figured that out soon enough myself, because, just then, the mountainside redoubt of the Mien warlord's lair came into sight.

The stronghold was well concealed, especially from the air. It consisted mainly of a large, open-air pavilion set on a rock outcrop at the side of a narrow ravine that appeared to be easily defended. It would be very hard to pick out from the air, because the columns that supported the thatched roof of the pavilion were the trunks of live jungle trees that widely spread their canopies over the whole complex.

As our truck came to a stop at the mouth of the ravine, I looked out, saw that and Kwei Lin and his most trusted cohorts were spread out along the low rock wall separating the pavilion from the cliff edge. I had no trouble picking out Kwei Lin; he stood head and shoulders above the rest of the Mien tribesmen and was as blond as either Gail or me, his golden hair flowing down to his shoulders in a full-bodied cascade of curls. It was immediately obvious why he was able to maintain his status as the guerilla band chief. Luck was with him just by virtue of his golden blond presence. It also was understandable why he had insisted on the reward that he had for accommodating the insertion of our team into China. He would perpetuate his myth of the golden leader of the Golden Triangle by mating with a blonde woman, while at the same time, he would be getting a taste of the world he'd left behind.

Kwei Lin was wearing the same indigo Chinese-style, close-fitting rough-fabric pants that came down to just below his knees and a loose-fitting crossover jacket made of the same material that the other men were wearing. But he was slimmer, taller, and more distinctly muscled than his adopted compatriots. Like his comrades, as well, all of his torso and arms that we could see were covered in an intricate design of blue tattooing that even ran up the side of his neck.

He spoke excellent French as we negotiated our business, but I never could discern whether he could speak English as well. I was careful not to ask him too many questions about his past, especially since he knew I was a direct agent of U.S. intelligence, and he didn't offer any personal information. It was clear that the Mien tribesmen would do anything he approved, and they seemed in awe of Gail, who just lounged coolly in a nearby rope sling, being as enticing as possible for Kwei Lin as she had been instructed to be, while the chieftain and I hashed out our agreement. For his part Kwei Line wasn't nearly as attentive to Gail's presence as his cohorts were; his attention was locked on me and what I was proposing.

We were able to strike a very acceptable bargain within a short time, and, as twilight descended, a couple of women were shuffling around and lighting small torches extending from the live columns but well away from the thatched ceiling.

Making quite clear that the U.S. government was quite pleased with the arrangement, I ceremoniously beckoned for Gail to come forward so that Kwei Lin could claim the sugaring of his deal. She languidly unfolded herself from the rope sling and floated over to the center to the pavilion, up to the edge of the table where Kwei Lin and I had spread our maps during the negotiations.

I had the interpreter announce to Kwei Lin that Gail would accommodate him for the night and was turning to return to the bottom of the ravine where a tent had been raised over the truck bed for the rest of my party to spend an uncomfortable night, when Kwei Lin spoke out in a commanding voice.

"He wants you to stay, Sir," the interpreter said, with a funny look on his face.

"Stay?" I asked dumbly.

"Yes. He wants you to make love to the blonde woman." the interpreter said in embarrassed tones. "He said he was promised two yellow hairs who would perform for him and his lieutenants."

"Two yellow hairs?" I said with a catch in my throat. "To perform? Here? Now."

"Yes, Sir, that's what he said. And I don't think he's negotiating about this."

Damn that Luther, I thought. So this was what he meant by my being perfect for the job. It was because I was a blond, although a silver blond in contrast to Gail's yellow blonde and Kwei Lin's golden hair. I wasn't on this mission because of any intelligence skill I had—just because I was blond. Well, I didn't mind fucking Gail, as long as she was good with the change in plans, and I wasn't that squeamish about doing it in front of these tribesmen, either.

In a short, whispered monologue, I explained the situation to Gail, whose only response was to reach around and unhook her halter top to much jabbering and oohing of appreciation from the gathered tribesmen, and to lay her back down on the top of the sturdy wooden table, with her butt cheeks on the rim. I stripped off my shirt and moved in between her legs and came down to her lips with mine. While we were kissing deeply, my hands were gliding over her breasts, rubbing and pinching her nipples, making them hard. I tongued my way down to them, and she arched her back for me in willing response. I was gathering up her skirt with my hands, bunching it up at her waist, showing Kwei Lin and his comrades that she was wearing nothing underneath. They oohed and awed and talked in rushed tones among themselves to see the golden yellow of her triangle.

My fingers entered her, searching for and finding her hooded clit and freeing it and making it hard. Gail was moaning for me, and my fingers were getting wet from her flow.

She had been running her fingers through my hair as I tongued her nipples, but she took them away and I heard her give a little grunt. I looked up, and saw that Kwei Lin was standing beside her head at another edge of the table. He was naked now, although he seemed clothed by the intricate webbing of dark tattooing all over his torso and arms, which extended down his thighs to his knees. He was holding an imposing, hard dick at the root, where curly yellow-gold hair pubic hair met the base of his cock, with one hand, and the back of Gail's head with the other. She was sucking him off, and both seemed to be enjoying the play. She had one hand wrapped around the hand he was guiding his cock with and the other palmed across his flat belly.

I kissed and tongued my way down Gail's belly and soon had my lips on the sweet lips to her golden triangle. My tongue searched beyond these lips until it found Gail's clit, and I sucked on that until it was hard and her pelvis started to undulate. I then let my tongue explore further into her wet, sweet-smelling canal. I had a thumb buried in her ass and I rotated that as Gail's hips strove to find my rhythm. My cock was hard and throbbing now, and I unbuckled and unzipped my pants and dropped them to the floor. I took my cock in my hand and rubbed it against her clit, while she trembled and moaned her appreciation and became wetter and wetter. Then I pushed my dick past her clit and into her tight, wet tunnel and glided up into her to the hilt until my silver-blond pubic hair intertwined with her golden yellow hair. I pumped her in short and long strokes, trying to match the rhythm of Kwei Lin's thrusts down her throat.

Our audience of Mien tribesmen was enthralled by the golden triangle that was performing a primeval dance of lust for them, and I could only suppose that Kwei Lin was piling up heaps of political capital with them for having brought them this spectacle.

I watched as Kwei Lin pulled away from Gail's mouth and then lost sight of him as he moved in behind me. I felt his hand come between my legs and his fingers inserting themselves alongside my stroking cock inside Gail's canal. He pulled my head to the side to meet his lips and gave me a long, lingering kiss. He then pushed me down onto Gail's chest with a strong hand in the small of my back, and Gail and I entwined our arms and allowed our tongues to duel with each other. She clearly was enjoying this double attention. And I was immensely enjoying the rubbing of her taunt nipples against mine.

Soon thereafter, I felt Kwei Lin's fingers, wet with Gail's flow, at my asshole, and he was fingering me, finger-fucking me in the ass. I barely had time to decide what, if anything, to do to counter this move, though, when the head of his dick, still wet from Gail's sucking, was pushing at the ring of my hole. I tried to raise up as he entered me with his big, thick cock, but my arms were entwined in Gail's and he was pushing firmly down on my back with his hand. Then he was in, past my sphincter, and I was groaning and gasping for air from the pain and stuffed sensation. He now had both hands pushing down on my shoulder blades.

It seemed to take forever for him to bury his rod up me to the hilt, but then my undulating ass walls were accommodating him, and the pleasure was beginning to overcome the pain. And I pumped Gail and Kwei Lin pumped me, and we all reached our orgasms nearly simultaneously. And the Mien tribesmen jabbered among themselves at the incredible good luck that the golden hairs were spinning out for them before their eyes, no doubt looking forward to a bumper opium crop this season as a result of our exertions.

Chapter Nine: Legend of Cowboy

All sorts of expatriate "characters" gravitated to Bangkok, Thailand, in the seventies and eighties, and none were more colorful than the man known simply as Cowboy. Cowboy was a six-and-a-half foot black American stud, who was said, alternately to be an American airman who, once assigned to Thailand, stayed there and, somewhat more romantically, to have been a pro basketball player of some note who had retreated to Bangkok in the face of possible charges for point shaving and racketeering. In Bangkok, Cowboy had built a small empire of girlie (and boy) bars in the Patpong tenderloin district, the most notable one of which was named, appropriately enough, Cowboy's. Later he moved his operations to a short street between Soi 21 and 23 Sukhumvit, which had been named for him and is still there today, providing the same entertainment venues it ever did.

There were a few legends about Cowboy beyond how he got to Thailand. One was that he had the biggest dick in Thailand, which was given some evidence by the women who buzzed around him looking very satisfied. The second was that he would fuck anything that moved, which was at least partially evidenced by the men who buzzed around him as well. And the third was that he never took off his signature ten-gallon hat, chaps, or spurs, even during sex.

Cowboy was one of the most happy-go-lucky, witty, and generous people in the international community, and those who knew him reacted well to him no matter how much effort they had to put into ignoring his past and his reputation.

A few months into my tour as an SR71 photoreconnaissance jet driver living in Bangkok, I decided I'd like to check out the legend of Cowboy. I joined the U.S. embassy's bowling league just because he was on it, and I got as close to his inner circle there as possible. Eventually, he invited me to come up and see him sometime at his flagship Cowboy's bar. As, at the time of the invitation, he had his hand under a table exploring my basket, I didn't have any illusions what his invitation entailed. This suited me just fine, of course, and I wasted no time in scooting over to Cowboy's to see him one afternoon in the next week.

When I walked into Cowboy's, I was told that Cowboy was in his office on the second floor and to go on up. Cowboy's office was a pretty good-sized room, with a desk and other office equipment at one end and a double bed with a red velour bedspread at the other end.

Cowboy was home, as was a dreamy-eyed woman with long, frizzed-up blonde hair and big tits. Cowboy was lying on the bed, feet pointed at me. He was wearing his ten-gallon hat and his boots with spurs, but that was all, so at least the part of the legend of the chaps was false. The blonde was sitting astride his pelvis, with her tits also pointed at me. I therefore couldn't check out the legend of the biggest dong in Thailand, at least for the moment, because the blonde was sitting on it.

She looked vaguely familiar to me, and it slowly dawned on me that she was the wife of one of the U.S. embassy's economic affairs officers. She'd bowled a 280 on the last league night, and, I understand, had gone out on a celebration binge and hadn't been seen for two days. It had taken me a few minutes to recognize her, because the economic affairs officer's wife I'd known had always been wearing clothes, and this woman was naked. Really nice tits, though.

When I walked in, Cowboy had his hands on her hips and was helping her to have a bouncy ride on his lap. They both seemed happy to see me, though, and Cowboy boomed out that I should feel free to strip down and come join them. He suggested that the woman might like to suck me off while she was getting her ride, and she seemed agreeable to this. So, I stripped down and went up on the bed with my knees straddling Cowboy's calves and my butt sitting on his boots. His spurs jangled quietly behind me.

Before the woman started to service me, I buried my face between her tits and did some exploration of those with my hands. That seemed to turn her on—or a bit more on than Cowboy had already turned her—and, after a while, she pushed me back on my haunches, and stretched forward and started giving my cock good head with her soft mouth.

Cowboy must have gotten bored with this, because after ten minutes or so of her slurping and me hardening, Cowboy asked me if I wanted to ride too. I said sure, not knowing what he had in mind, but being game for about anything until I was able to fully check out this legend thing. When I had voiced my agreement, his big hands came around from either side of the woman's chest, and he cupped her tits and pulled her back onto his torso, which brought her pelvis up.

Wonders of wonders! Cowboy was in her asshole, not her cunt. Her pouty little cunt was sitting right there, begging for attention from me. So I just slid up Cowboy's thighs and drilled my hard seven inches into her. She was writhing and moaning, having a good time being double stuffed. She took my head in both of her hands and brought our lips together, and I kissed her deeply, thinking that was only polite considering how deeply I was fucking her. All three of us were riding and bucking and rotating, sometimes in synch, sometimes not, but always in ways that gave all three of us pleasure.

While I was kissing the woman, Cowboy let loose of her tits and started to play with mine. I liked the attention fine. He even managed to get my nipples aligned with those of the woman, and he did some rubbing and pinching together that was driving us both crazy.

I came out of my kiss with the woman and dove beside her head and found Cowboy's mouth. We did a battle of the tongues that was more invigorating than what the woman and I had been doing. She was a fine ride, but I knew which side my bread was buttered on.

I felt the woman's pelvis being pushed into mine, so I put my hands under her butt cheeks and pulled her up with me, as I went up on my knees. I heard a long slurping noise as Cowboy came out of her ass and pulled himself up toward the head of the bed from under us. The woman and I went back down on the bed and she held her legs out briefly and then brought her heels to the back of my calves and massaged them while I pumped her. She was making little mewing sounds.

Cowboy was behind me. He was lathering up his cock with KY, and I took a peek. That part of the legend probably was true. He was longer, if not thicker, than anyone else I'd seen in Bangkok. His dick was a darker brown than the rest of his body and had a big pinkish-brown helmet on it. I started my own little mewing sounds at that point.

He took me by the hips and just lifted me up off and out of the woman and I dug my knees into the bed again to prop myself up. Cowboy's mouth went to my asshole and he tongued and kissed me there. The woman slipped out from underneath me and reversed herself and came back under. She took my cock in her mouth and restarted the stimulation there. She played with my balls with her hands, until Cowboy's cock was engaged and nearby, and then she gave his cock root and balls attention. I lowered myself on her and spent my time servicing her g-spot with my tongue, holding her gyrating pelvis within some sort of limits with my hands dug into her butt cheeks. Her tits felt good bobbing against my belly.

Cowboy stopped licking my butt and applied some KY there and then entered me, and entered me, and entered me, and entered me. I didn't think his dong would ever stop sliding up into me. And when he was well in, he started plowing me really good at a depth I didn't remember ever doing any entertaining before. With her soprano, my tenor, and his bass, we had a real good harmony of sighs and moaning going there for a while.

After a good fifteen minutes, Cowboy pulled out of me, sort of pushed me off to the side and turned the woman around to finish his fuck and shoot off his load in her cunt. I didn't mind, because by then, I was drilling his ass to my own climax.

So, other than the chaps, the Cowboy legend pretty much held up to scrutiny.

Chapter Ten: Family Day on the Pool Table

I had always thought that about the only thing you could do on a pool table was play pool, but the Taylor brothers went to great length and depth to teach me otherwise.

I'd met the three brothers on the beach at Pataya resort in Thailand. Their family owned a hotel construction company and was making money hand over fist in throwing up fancy hotels in downtown Bangkok and at the Pataya and Hua Hin beach resorts. All three brothers, in their late twenties and early thirties worked in the family firm, mostly on the construction sites themselves, which had helped them to stay trim and to bulk up nicely.

I met them on the sand below their fancy beach house in Pataya one Saturday afternoon. I was just passing by, walking the water line, when they called out to me and invited me to play doubles volleyball with them for a while. They lacked a fourth, and I was the first one who came along, I guess, who they figured was athletic enough to give them a workout. And, as it turned out, I really did give all three of them a good workout before the afternoon was through.

I was happy to play volleyball with them, because all three of them were real easy to look at, all bulked up in small Speedos that showed off very promising baskets. I'd already seen one of them, the younger brother, Randy, at a cast party after a play in Bangkok, which had ended as a major male fuck fest, and where I'd been bottomed twice, so I knew they—or Randy, at least—knew that I had been fucked before—as I knew which way his wind blew as well. Volleyball is a contact sport, and there was a lot of touching and rubbing, which is nice when the bodies are hard and well-cut, which pretty much defined the Taylor brothers.

After an hour of volleyball and beer, Randy invited me up to the house to shower off and to play some pool during the heat of the day in the area under their house, which was raised on stilts. I accepted, and we all showered at an outdoor shower on the path leading up to the house.

I didn't know how to play pool all that well, and when it was my turn to stroke the ball, Randy got behind me to show me how to hold the cue. Everything just sort of developed quickly from there. He was close in back of me. I could feel his basket against my butt, and I knew from the bulge I felt there that that he was getting really interested in me. He had his arms around me, holding my arms on the cue to show me how to hold it, his chest touching my back, and his chin on my shoulder, and I just turned my face to him, and he came in for a deep kiss. The time of my tour in Bangkok was the anything goes period of my life, so I just went with the kiss.

Then he had his hands all over my chest and nipples and belly and down onto the basket of my Speedo. He flipped me around and lifted me on the table, pushing the pool balls aside, and laid me on my back with my butt at the edge of the table. Then he went for my tits with this tongue. I have large aureoles around my nipples, and they are an especially sensitive point of sexual stimulation for me, so I got all hot and bothered quickly as he thumbed, stroked, pinched, and sucked on my nipples.

I let him know that I liked what he was doing to me, and he said he'd figured that out already, as he'd seen a big Swede doing this to me at the party in Bangkok, and he'd wanted to do it to me ever since. The Swede had stuffed my ass really good with a juicy Swedish sausage too, so I knew where Randy was headed with all of this.

"You gonna treat me right?" I murmured.

"I'm going to fuck you to heaven," he answered in a low, throaty voice.

After giving my tits a good workout, he tongued his way down my chest, gave me some head, and then dove for opening up my asshole with tonguing, kissing, and licking. When he was satisfied that he had me moistened up and opened, he pushed me on up the table and climbed on top with me. He knelt, with his knees under the small of my back, holding my left leg wrapped around his waist, and my right leg being lifted up with my calf on his chest. I was arching my back, with my head and shoulders resting on the surface of the pool table.

"Now, god, now," I muttered.

I had a good view of him entering me with a supercock. I did some groaning, heavy breathing, and slapping of the table top with my hands as his cock slowly disappeared into my hole.

"Shit, yes," I cried out.

Randy's brothers, Andy and Frank, had just been standing around and watching us with big grins on their faces, but when Randy had run his cock all the way in and had begun to pump me, the older brother, Frank, stripped off his Speedo.

"Got to get me some of that too," I heard him exclaim.

"Oh, shit yes. Both of you," I answered.

He hopped up on the table and straddled my head with his knees and started eating out my cock. He had a nice eight-incher and heavy balls, so I gave those head.

Randy came pretty quickly, and pulled out of me and hopped off the pool table. Frank had saved his load, and, when Randy was gone, Frank flipped me over on my belly, straddled me on his knees with his calves on either side of my thighs, lifted my pelvis up with his hands on my hips, and drilled my ass with a cock that must have been about the same size as Randy's. And I'd been able to handle Randy without much trouble. With Randy, though, I'd managed to stretch my legs and butt cheeks to accommodate his size. But Frank held my thighs in tight together and he really filled and stretched my ass canal as he entered my tightened asshole and slid and drilled up to his root. I'd been working his cock while Randy was fucking me, so he came almost as quickly as Randy had.

"Good as Randy," he asked through heavy breathing.

"Don't ask," I whimpered. "Give me more."

But it obviously was going to be Andy, the middle brother's, turn to give me more. He was the hunkiest of all and had an even longer cock than either of his brothers did. And when he came up on the table, I saw that he'd enhanced that. He had some sort of sheath covering his cock that had little rubber knobby and spiking things all up and down it and it was ribbed.

"Oh shit, oh shit," I said with a groan. But Andy laughed when I grabbed my ankles and raised and spread my legs, welcoming him.

Andy brushed my hands away, though and turned me on my right side, with my right leg bent. He came in behind me and took my left leg and pulled it out and over his body. He was holding my torso up with his right arm around my back. His right hand was cupping my right breast, and he was thumbing my nipple. I turned my head to him, and he came in for a deep kiss as his sheathed cock slowly entered my ass, which was now open, loose, and well-lubricated with the cum from both of his brothers. I felt every knob and spike and rib on his cock sheath rub at my prostate and canal walls, as he slowly pushed in nine inches or more. He filled me a good bit deeper than either of his brothers had managed. As he started his pumping action, his lips went to my left nipple, and he gathered it, big aureole and everything, into his mouth and started to suck. I writhed and bucked under him, joining in the rhythm of his fuck. I got my hand on my dick and was stroking myself, when Randy came back up on the table and swallowed my cock and took my cum when I shot my load.

I never did learn how to play pool. I might have, but old man Taylor had arrived during my last skewering and had stripped, sat in a rattan chair, and stroked himself while I was servicing his oldest son and being serviced by his youngest.

Frank unloaded up my ass canal, and then, before I knew it was going to happen, Randy and Frank had delivered me to their dad's lap. He lifted me off his lap and had me place my knees on the wide rattan arms of the chair, facing him, and he cupped my butt cheeks in his big, rough hands, and tongued and kissed my belly and balls for a while and then sucked me off. And he was really good at giving head.

After I'd come, he sat me back down in his lap, held me by my hips, and skewered my ass with a cock that wasn't nearly as long as any of his son's dicks but that was considerably thicker and had a lot more experience behind it in how to drive a man wild with rotations and various rhythms of pumping. My left leg was hooked on his shoulder, and my right leg was out to the side of the chair. I arched my back, and he brought his mouth back down to my belly and chest, while he pumped me in short strokes from below and got his hand down there and rotated his cock around in my canal. I made little appreciative purring noises for him. I knew the father was far richer than any of the sons. And he was probably harder muscled than any of them too; I certainly felt his most important muscle harder than I had with any of his sons. I'd already discovered that I liked to be fucked by men in their forties or fifties better than in their twenties—as long as they were superb shape, which the senior Taylor was.

He must not have liked the leverage he was getting, because he rose from the chair on powerful legs and marched back over to the pool table. I had my arms and legs wrapped around him, his hands were under my butt, and he managed to keep his dong buried in my ass. At the table, I wound up right where I had started with Randy—me bent over the table on my chest, and the old man pumping me from behind. At one point, he had me take my legs up with my heels on the edge of the table and my ass waving way out for him, and he swung me against the pressure of his cock, but that got a little much both of us, and he had me stand back down on one leg, with the other one stretched up on the table, and he sort of side split me from the side, the slide of his cock stroking me at a new, arousing angle.

And, boy, did he have stamina. He pumped longer than all of his sons together. A real family man, he seemed to be immensely enjoying his cum mixing with the semen of all three of his offspring in my ass canal, and nearly a half hour after he'd begun his expedition trip up my ass, he shoot off his load inside me.

I had a really good time, but I'm just as glad that there weren't any other Taylor brothers or a funny uncle or two visiting Pataya to service. The joke was sort of on them, though. I had fucked Mrs. Taylor—and we'd had orgasmed together once for each of her sons—in a suite in the Montien Hotel in Bangkok just two days before this little party. When I had walked by their place on the beach, I'd actually been hoping it was her who invited me in to party.

Chapter Eleven: Doubling Bets

I should have known that the sneaky Dutchman had all the angles figured when he suckered us into betting against a myth in the Men Only back room at Cowboy's Bar in Bangkok's Patpong district. He waited until the third revolution of the happy hour clock—when we were all soused and sluggish—and then entered with a boy-built Thai. I recognized the Thai immediately as a champion bantam-weight kick boxer from the arena over by Lumpini Park. Knowing the Thai, I figured he probably was a lot closer to thirty than he was to twenty, but he wasn't much over five feet tall and was skinny as a rail. All corded sinew, though, and I'd seen him put opponents in the hospital over in the ring. He still had all of his facial features where they belonged and was quite well turned out in looks, so it's obvious he'd been able to defend himself successfully.

Those of us holding up the bar couldn't isolate—even when we revisited the issue several days later—who exactly brought up the question of whether the legend that two guys could fuck another one in the ass simultaneously was fact or fiction. But it must have been the Dutchman. He must have had it all planned before he brought the Thai kick boxer into Cowboy's. Having seen it done—but not with such as this slim Thai—I stood by in amusement.

It came down to the boys at the bar against the Dutchman. My drinking companions all said it was a myth, and the Dutchman asked us if we wanted to take up bets on that. Suckers that my friends were, They did. We all put our heads together, without me saying anything to dissuade them, and even thought we'd put one over on him, when one of us had the presence of mind to stipulate that we could pick the cocks that would be buried. That stipulation accepted by the Dutchman, my friends went around our group taking the time and effort to do some comparing and measuring. The Dutchman even let us check out the Thai's hole on a surface inspection, and led my friends into doubling the stakes when we saw there was nothing especially slack about the Thai's backdoor.

I came up second longest and thickest, so I was picked as one of the house champions. Dennis, a news agency journalist, who was a good fuck buddy of mine, got highest honors, which pleased me; we'd taken turns with each other as top and bottom, and I enjoyed either position with him.

After Dennis and I had stripped down, I was pleased to see that the Thai was showing that he thought this was all a good idea. He was all smiles and winks and lustful looks. It should have been another signal for my drinking buddies when he didn't seem to mind what was going on—but for all we knew, he hadn't been clued in on the plan at that point yet—or, indeed, just didn't understand English very well. We cleared a space in the center of the room and someone found a cot mattress from somewhere in the depths of Cowboy's back establishment, and we had our arena.

Dennis, the Thai, and I engaged in a good half hour of three-way feeling and kissing, stroking, cocksucking, and greasing ourselves up lavishly with lube to get us all in the mood and to get Dennis and me lengthened and thickened to the point where we assumed our bet was well covered. In time, though, I found myself on my back on the mattress and the Thai straddling my hips with his thighs. And then he was settling on my cock. Dennis had a hand under there, fingers wrapped around my cock and rotating my dick head in what felt like a tight ass opening. But then the Thai arched his back above me, settled his pelvis, and he was coming down on my cock, swallowing it with his ass, the muscles of his canal walls undulating along the sides of my cock as he settled down into my lap. He was driving me crazy down there, and I managed to tell Dennis between gasps what was happening. The boxer had magic ass muscles and was going to make me come and start going flaccid before Dennis got his cock into position.

The Thai was grinning above me, going for my nipples with his strong fingers, trying to bring me past the brink.

Forewarned, however, Dennis pushed the Thai's chest down toward mine, tipping his hips up, and I felt the giant mushroom head of Dennis's cock at the base of my dick where it was encased by the Thai's asshole. Dennis was grunting mightily from the effort to enter the Thai, and the Thai, his face very close to mine, was registering pain in his eyes and panting with exertion himself.

But slowly, ever so slowly, Dennis's cock was sliding in, and I felt its warm, hard, yet pliable skin pushing in on the underside of my own cock. All three of us were straining now from the effort. But somehow the Thai took us both. He reached a point where we were both beyond the entry-level of muscles in his ass, and I could see the transition in his eyes from overriding pain and some sense of uncertainty to triumph and "ride me hard" lust.

We'd lost the bet to the Dutchman, who was showing no pain or exertion at all as he walked around the circle of oglers, pulling in cash. But, without the exchange of audible signals, Dennis and I managed to agree to get a good ride for the money. We started pumping the Thai in counter pistoning that produced arousing friction I've never felt in a corn-hole encounter since. And good sport and magnificently conditioned athlete that he was, the Thai went with us and we all bucked to near-simultaneous ejaculations.

So, now, whenever I hear anyone pooh, pooh the idea that double penetration can even be done, I just smile a little smile and remember how I got more value in losing a bet in the backroom of Cowboy's bar than I'd have gotten if I and my drinking buddies had won.

I got a bonus that night. I'd been working up to offering myself to Dennis, but I hadn't been sure he'd be interested. After our little performance with the Thai kick boxer, Dennis picked up the cot mattress that had been brought from the back of Cowboy's and, giving me a meaningful look, asked if I wanted to help him return it to the back room. I most certainly did.

I was purring as I lay under him and grunted at his deep thrusts and he murmured how sexy it had felt for us to be inside the kick boxer together and how he'd wanted to fuck me for the longest time.

Chapter Twelve: The Darling

"I'm going to take you to the Darling tonight."

I froze. I'd been chatting with three other guys on the sectional sofa in the conversation pit, not even aware that the major had reentered the house. I was studiously avoiding thinking of where he was. Otherwise I wouldn't have been in this conversation group at all. I normally tried to stay well away from these three. The three pansies we had termed them behind their backs—all three of the limp-wristed type, all affiliated in some way with the music and theater world of the expatriate community in Thailand, even though two of them were Thai. They only went with men as a threesome, joined at the hip. There were men here, though, who enjoyed the novelty of having three at a time. I wasn't one of them. And, thank god, neither was the major. As far as I knew.

I didn't keep track of who the major was fucking. He wasn't the kind who wanted anyone hanging on him like that. As long as he was fucking me, I just let that question be. The major. That's what we all called him then, and now, decades later, I no longer can recall what his real name was, even though Thailand was not the last post where we met up.

"I'm going to take you to the Darling tonight," he said in that rich baritone voice of his, as I looked down to see the strong, chocolate-brown hand he had rested on my forearm. He had leaned down to speak in my ear. I looked up into the eyes of the three pansies. Their litany of whining complaints and snippy gossip had been interrupted and they were all staring beyond my head, over my shoulder, at the heavily muscled barrel chest tapering down to the flat, hard belly and slim waist of the major's. He had come to the party in just low-slung jeans and sandals, knowing that all eyes would follow him around the room. I suspect he'd done that this evening because he'd planned what he was going to say to me—what he was going to do with me—and he wanted me to know that if I didn't go with him, he could have his pick of nearly every other man at the party.

He also, I'm sure, knew how aroused I'd be just to see him walk into the room—and to know that he fucked me.

I saw the eyes of the three pansies slit, almost as if in unison, and their sharp little tongues flicking out to wet their lips in arousal and, could it be, in some remembrance of shared experience. Yes, it could, I guessed. I wanted to think that the major wouldn't have been interested in them, but I claimed no knowledge—or hold—over what the major liked or had done beyond putting his brand on me. I had visions of him fucking all three of them, in quick succession, if only for the variety and exercise that entailed.

"Yes, if that's what you want," I whispered.

"That's what I want," he murmured, running his hands into the deep arm holes of the athletic T I was wearing and cupping my pecs. I leaned my head back onto his sternum and turned my face up to him as he kissed me with those thick, sensuous lips. When I tilted my head back down, I saw that the three pansies were hanging on every movement, their envy barely shielded. I heard a collective sigh as he stood, pulling his hands back from my chest.

"One more drink and we'll leave," he said. And then he was gone.

"If that's what you want," I repeated. But he was already gone, and the three pansies were already leaning into each other, pointedly ignoring me, and resuming their gossiping.

He had won. The major had beaten me. It had been a three-month struggle, but he'd finally gotten me to agree to go to the Darling with him. This was the first time he'd flatly told me I was going to go there with him. It's probable that, if he had said it in declarative earlier, I would have obediently agreed. I doubt I could ever flatly say no to a command from the major. He fucked me like no one had ever done before—nor, as far as I can remember, ever since. He was built like a horse, was a power driver, and was so strong that he manipulated me like I was a rag doll. And I loved muscular, demanding black men.

He'd always phrased it as a question before, and I had begged off, for what I thought were good reasons. But tonight it was a declaration, and, coming on the heels of the news he'd given me earlier out on the terrace by the pool, I couldn't say no.

"I've gotten my orders," he'd said. "It's back Stateside."

I paused for a few moments for that to sink in. He was holding me in his arms, and I'm sure he could feel me trembling. I had his jeans unbuttoned and was giving him a hand job, assuming he'd take me to one of the loungers around the pool and fuck me. We wouldn't be the only ones doing it. He liked to fuck publicly. He liked having an audience gather around him while he was showing his prowess and displaying that thick ten-by-two incher of his. And I didn't mind it when it was him—but only him. With him, I was aroused at the thought of all those men gathered around us, wishing that they were getting what I was getting.

I unbuttoned and unzipped my shorts and pushed them and my briefs down to my ankles. I didn't want to think about what he said. If I didn't react to it, maybe it wouldn't be true. I didn't know what I'd do in Bangkok without him. Well, I'd continue to find big men to fuck me, of course. There was no shortage of offers. But for nearly a year he'd been at the base of those I coupled with. I compared all of the men I went with to him, and all had come up shorter or thinner, or with less drive or inferior technique. I lifted a leg and hooked it on his hip. I used the hand I'd been jacking him off with to move his cock to below my ball sack. I moaned as his cock head rubbed across my perineum.

"Fuck me here, standing," I murmured.

"Did you hear me? I have ongoing orders. I'll be leaving Bangkok."

"I always thought I'd be the first to go," I answered. "Agency tours are shorter than those in the military."

"I know," he answered. His hands were palming my buttocks. I thought he was going to do as I asked. Just lift me up and set me on his cock, standing. If he did that, I would arch back toward the terrace, palming the rocky surface with my hands, giving those inside the house, beyond the wide glass doors, the full effect of the fuck—his rippling chest muscles in full view, his straining arm muscles holding my pelvis to him as he fucked down into me. That would please him and those in the house too—and thus, I would be pleased as well. And I could try to dismiss what he'd said from my mind.

He wouldn't go farther toward taking me right there and then, though. He just held me there, motionless, against his chest.

"You know there's something I want you to do with me. I'll be leaving soon. I will be disappointed if I leave without that. It could be your farewell present to me."

"The Darling. You want to bring that up again."

He just gazed at me, expectantly, until I broke down and spoke again.

"We've discussed this before. It's too close . . . and it's one thing with you, but with another—"

"It's what I want."

I broke away from him then, pulled my shorts up, and retreated into the house. Everyone else I walked by was coupling up already, so I had nowhere to go to fold into a conversation— except for the conversation pit. The three pansies had taken up residence there and no one had come by yet to take them all, giggling and wiggling their butts, up the stairs to the bedroom level. I sat on the sofa near them and turned my attention—or pretended to—toward them. They, in turn, pretended that I was part of their conversation. They didn't try too hard, though. They saw me as competition. I wouldn't be taking them upstairs, but the next man who drifted over sniffing for some tail, might choose me instead of them.

The minutes ticking by without anything happening—especially since I had no idea at all what I wanted to happen—were excruciating. Even though I couldn't see him, since I had pointedly positioned my back to the door out onto the terrace, my mind was trying to trace where the major was, what he was doing. Had he, out of pique, decided to punish me by pointing to another man and pinning him to a lounge cushion with his cock? If so, most of the men at the party would have gone with him with a smile and a sigh. And, if so, I would deserve it.

I had what I thought were good reasons for my reluctance. The Darling was too close to my apartment—at the head of Soi 12 Sukhumvit. My apartment was farther down the same street. There was only one entrance into Soi 12, and it went right by the forecourt of the Darling. Every time I walked home from the embassy, I had to pass the Darling. And nearly every time I did, there were both men and women out in front of the Darling, soliciting. I would be recognized in the Darling, I had every reason to presume. Beyond that, there was what the major wanted me to do in the Darling. It was one thing to let him fuck me in public—I had become accustomed to that and even, now, was aroused by that. What he wanted in the Darling, though, was something entirely different.

So deep in thoughtful concern was I that I didn't hear him approach.

"I am going to take you to the Darling tonight."

He was leaning over me on the sofa in the conversation pit.

"Yes, if that's what you want."

* * * *

He obviously had thought ahead. A black Mercedes with tinted windows was outside the house when we left. He handed me into the backseat and climbed in beside me. He said nothing to the driver, who apparently already knew where we were going.

As we drove across Bangkok in traffic that still, this late in the evening, was door handle to door handle on the clogged streets, the major put an arm around my back, tilted my head to his with his other hand, and took me into a kiss with those thick lips of his. His hand moved down to the waistband of my shorts. He unbuttoned and unzipped me and pulled my half-hard cock out.

I whimpered for him, moaning a "please," that he knew was not a request for him to stop.

His hand dipped farther down, his fingers moving between my thighs and across my perineum, the tips of his middle finger coming to rest on the rim of my hole. I rolled my hips up to give him better purchase and sighed. One of my hands involuntarily went down and covered the back of his hand, holding him there, wanting him inside me.

He buried the fist of his other hand in my hair and pulled my head back. His face was very close to mine. I knew what he wanted now. He wanted to watch the expression on my face change while he had his way with me.

I heard him grunt, and recognizing that he didn't want me to reach for him in this instance, I just relaxed, took my hand away from his, and let him play my body. He always wanted to be in full control.

As he slowly worked first one and then two and, finally, three fingers into my channel, I ached to put my hand on my engorging cock and stroke it to relief. But I knew he wouldn't want that and would brush the hand away—and in doing so would have to pull his fingers out of me. I didn't want him to do that.

I began to moan and move my pelvis on his hand as his middle finger found and began to play my prostate.

"Please, daddy," I moaned. "Let me ride you."

"Later," he said.

I groaned as he continued to play me.

"Please. My cock. Let me . . ."

That was the signal he was waiting for. He withdrew his fingers from my hole and wrapped his fist tightly around my cock and slow pumped me until I gave a little cry, tightened up, and ejaculated.

He gave a low, throaty laugh and lowered his lips to my cock and cleaned me up.

* * * *

The Mercedes pulled into the forecourt and almost all the way up to the front door, where the light would have been very dim if it weren't for the frenetic glow of the orange neon sign flashing over the entrance announcing that we had arrived at the Darling. The driver opened the rear door and the major hustled me quickly from the backseat of the car into the entry, where we were met by a giant of a man who was bare-chested and bare footed and wearing a striped silk sarong around his waist.

"This is Boonsri. I told you about him," the major told me as the Thai giant turned and ushered us deeper into the bowels of the building.

And indeed the major had told me about Boonsri. Most tend to believe that Thai men are small, willowy figures, and many are. But some are big, heavily muscled men—nearly as stately as the major himself. Boonsri was one of those Thai.

The major had told me several times as he spun out a dream of his that this Boonsri was going to fuck me and the major was going to watch.

We had entered the Darling, the Darling Massage Parlor. In Thailand massage parlors are brothels. If you want minimal massaging leading to sex, you went to a place like the Darling. If you wanted both a good massage and sex, you joined an expensive gym. If you only wanted a good massage, people would wonder why you bothered to come to Thailand at all.

When the major had first told me that he wanted to take me to the Darling and I had begged off, I'd said I would certainly go to a massage parlor with him if that was what he wanted, but it would need to be one other than the Darling. That was too close to home. My wife and children knew as well as I did what happened in the Darling that we all had to pass each time we left our apartment compound or returned to it. But none of us openly discussed what the Darling was all about or wanted to get anywhere close to talking about whether I'd go to such a place—even though it was given as natural that well-heeled Thai men frequented such places even if they were happily married. And I wanted to keep it that way. The first unguarded mention by anyone that they'd seen me at the Darling, and the whole life and career I had so carefully constructed would have collapsed upon itself.

"It has to be the Darling," he said.

"Why?" I asked.

"Because Boonsri, the man I want to share you with, is at the Darling. He's indentured there. He can't go anywhere else."

"And it has to be him?"

"Oh, yes, it has to be him," the major had answered.

And here we were. When I saw Boonsri I was even more apprehensive than I'd been when the major had described him in the abstract.

The Thai giant turned and moved into the interior of the windowless building. The major took my elbow in a firm grip, and we followed the slapping sandals and the hem of the striped sarong on the polished wood floor. We were moving toward a room with a bright light and the recorded and amplified sound of a whiny Thai songstress singing to a half-toned stringed instrument. When we walked through the door and into this space, it proved to be yet another corridor. but the walls into the rooms adjoining the corridor were glass panels. On one side of the corridor, behind the glass, erotically clad women were sitting and reclining on couches and primping for a few men standing in the corridor who were, with the help of a Darling attendant, making their choices. In the other glass-fronted room on the other side of the corridor were the minimally dressed men and boys. There were more women than men on offer, and most of the attention in the corridor was focused on them, but a few men were turned toward the window looking in on the men and boys too. On both sides of the corridor, the men and women behind the glass were playing up to the men in the corridor, each vying for attention and selection.

Eyes followed us as we moved through the corridor, with most of them, of course, focused on the major. But not a few of the women and men behind the glass were primping for me as well.

I kept my head down, watching the hem of Boonsri's sarong as much as I could as we moved through the corridor. I didn't want anyone to recognize me on the days I walked by the Darling on my way to and from my apartment. The major was sensitive to me on this, and, indeed, seemed to have conveyed the need for stealth to the Thai giant before we arrived.

We went through another door and were in a stair hall. We followed Boonsri up one flight and then half way down another corridor, past a series of closed doors. The sounds coming from behind these doors left little doubt what was happening there. He turned and opened a door looking much like the rest and stood aside, beckoning the major and me to enter a small, mirror-walled room with a massage table in the center and a couple of straight chairs and a table at the side. I began to tremble as I saw that the table had packets of condoms, bottles of lubricant and massage oil, and various sex toys and restraints neatly arranged on the top of it. An alarm clock was also sitting on the table, but, slightly to my surprise, Boonsri didn't set the timer. This was my first indication that this would not be a rushed assignation.

At Boonsri's direction, both the major and I stripped down and piled our clothes on the same straight chair. When we turned around, Boonsri had loosened the knot on his sarong, let it fall, and was neatly folding it up as well. I gasped at the sight of his equipment. He was erect, leaving little question what service he would be performing for me—or that he would enjoy doing it.

He motioned for me to climb up on the massage table and lay down on my back. The major took a straight chair, reversed it, and straddled its seat. He folded his arms on the top of the chair's back, with his cock hanging down the back of the chair under the lowest rung, and urged Boonsri to start the show.

Boonsri was a legitimate masseur and was very good at his job—at all of his jobs: working my muscles, working my throat, and working my channel. He massaged my extremities in a deep-tissue workout and then my chest and torso muscles, relentlessly working his way to the center, and doing it so sensually that I was sighing for him and mellowing out.

As the major sat there and watched, the Thai took possession of my cock with his hand and slow pumped me until I had come for him. Then he pulled me forward on the table, with my head lolling off the edge. He was working my temples with his fingers, nearly putting me to sleep, when I felt the head of his cock at my lips and I opened my mouth and throat to him.

As was the case when I deep-throated the major in this position, I need do nothing but open as wide as possible for him and try not to choke.

He slowly face fucked me until the major requested a change in positions, and then he had me roll over on my front and gave an equally deep-tissue massage, moving toward a conclusion with his greased fingers invading my channel and massaging my prostate to my second coming. I turned my face to the major to see that he was masturbating himself and fully enjoying the performance. Boonsri finished me, taking a good half hour to do so, by climbing the table, straddling my hips, skewering my ass with a thick cock, arching my torso back in a full Nelson hold that pinned my arms above my head, and rocking back and forth to work my channel with his digging cock.

I was moaning and thoroughly exhausted when Boonsri had come and climbed off the table. With a groan, I turned over and started to sit up. But now it was the major's turn. He rose from his chair, walked over to the table, grabbed my ankles, and split my legs wide, causing me to collapse onto my back. I arched my back and cried out and moaned as he, longer and thicker and more strongly stroking than Boonsri, took me more roughly and completely than the Thai giant had.

The major took his time with me, and as exhausted as I was, I just lay there, tongue lolling, holding my legs as wide as possible to be able to take him, and luxuriated in the fuck of my favorite lover.

I wasn't in any way angry with the major for wanting to share me and to watch another man fuck me. The major had been good to me, and now he was leaving. Nothing would be the same after that. Anything I could do to show him how I had appreciated what he'd done for, with, and to me, I would do.

When the major was done, having folded me in his arms and rocked me like a baby into his explosive orgasm, I climbed down from the massage table and started to move toward the chair holding my clothes. But the major wrapped his arms around me and leaned me over the table surface. He motioned to Boonsri to return and to slide inside me and resume taking me from the rear. And then the major mounted the table, knelt, forced his knees under my chest and guided his cock between my lips.

I heard him murmur, "We have just begun," and I moaned in resignation, knowing that he wasn't lying to me.

* * * *

Six months later, the major still had not shipped out, and I began to suspect that he had made his reassignment orders up just to get me to agree to go to the Darling with him. I never brought the subject up, though. I held my breath and took as much enjoyment as I could from him still being in Bangkok—and with me when he wanted to be.

He never asked me again to go with him to the Darling, however. When he asked me whether I had enjoyed Boonsri's cocking, I had told him the truth.

Chapter Thirteen: Director's Couch

I often did things backwards in life. The old Hollywood adage goes that many a starlet—and we can add many a leading man, now that the cat is out of the closet on that—got their film career break by the audition they did on the director's or producer's couch. In my case, however, I got the part before the director had me taking direction under him on his couch.

I had been a child actor on stage and in a few movies before I went off to the university, having chosen to study international relations rather than drama or film making after a less-than-sterling screen test and a somewhat pessimistic assessment of my chances in Hollywood. I did get into male modeling while I was in college, though, and this double backed to a few minor roles on stage and bad movies as the young stud next door or in the background on the beach. When I got involved in flying supersonic spy jets as a sidestep from a war I didn't really agree with or want to see up front and in person, I was shipped off to Bangkok, Thailand. With that remote posting, I assumed that the film road not taken was now a dead-end to me.

As luck would have it, though, I found it even easier to fall into stage and screen roles when I arrived in Southeast Asia. Many movies were being filmed there, and casting directors relied on local actors for minor or background roles rather than facing the expense of bringing big casts in from the States. Thus it was that shortly before my first tour in Thailand was over, I found myself in some background crowd scenes and minor script editing work on the film, *The Deerhunter.* I had no idea at the time that this would be an Academy Award contender, or I would have fought my way to the front of set. However, I still must have performed my tasks on the movie reasonably well, because the casting director of that asked me if I'd be interested in taking some time off and being in Hawaii for a couple of weeks and work as an extra in a popular Hawaii-based police detective television show.

Hmmm, the question whether I would like a couple of expense-paid weeks in Hawaii working on a TV production. Not much of a question, right? And this fit right in with my schedule to be transferred back to the States for a short tour in preparation to what would be an even shorter tour flying SR71s out of Okinawa.

So, a few weeks later, in a prolonged stopover in Hawaii en route to a particularly snowy and slushy winter in Washington, D.C., I found myself as tiny swimsuited eye candy at beach bar background scenery for a couple of episodes of a Hawaii police detective show. I might have had a line or two in one of the episodes, but I can't really remember if I did.

This, after already having been cast in a TV production, was where my path crossed with the director destined to couch me under his personal and intense direction. He was a British director who specialized in sophisticated, sparkling-dialogued— and highly successful—spy and amateur detective stories both previously and subsequently to the tropical island interlude; he had been brought in to give the Hawaii show a needed kick in the butt to a more elevated viewer share. He was a handsome, charismatic figure—a good fifteen years older than me—with a spiffy English accent and a quick mind and tongue. He had left his wife back in the UK, and my wife had gone ahead to our Washington assignment. He liked to party and I liked to party, and the whole cast of the television show worked by day and partied at night.

Early in my stint on the television show, as may have been inevitable, I got half plastered at one of the cast's blowouts, and the director took me back to his hotel suite and banged me all night long.

He gave me fair warning, of course. He gave me the eye at the party, and I was flattered. And as we were going up in the elevator to his room—with me too far gone on bourbon and cokes to have any idea what we were even doing in his hotel—he was blunt and straightforward in his approach.

"There's no place you need to be tonight, is there?" he asked.

"Umm, no, I don't think so," I responded. I couldn't really be sure if I had promised to be someplace else. I'd already hooked up with one of the lighting guys and been fucked by him in some brush off the set on a Hawaiian beach, but I had too much of a buzz on to remember whether I'd agreed to wind up with him tonight or not. But this was the director—The Director—and if he wanted me to be here tonight, I was going to be here tonight.

"Good," he said when I had responded, "because, if you don't mind, I am going to fuck that scrumptious body of yours all night." I, of course, don't remember his exact words, but he had something sexy and seductive to say about my body in that defenses-melting British accent of his—and I did have a really fine body, so I naturally didn't think his request—or more of a statement of intent—was either unusual or off-putting.

I have no idea what answer I gave him, but it didn't stop us from arriving at his door, and once the door was closed behind us, from him pushing me to my knees and presenting a very nice cock against my lips for attention and preparation. I didn't normally do a lot of cocksucking, but this was The Director—and he'd asked very politely if he could do me.

He had been a gymnast and then a stunt man before directing stunts and then full productions, and I was to quickly find that he also was fast on the reload. So, I got had in a lot of very interesting positions that first night.

When he'd hardened up, he just pushed me to the floor on my belly, tore my clothes off, and ate out my ass until I was writhing on his carpet. I cried out appreciatively when he entered me from behind with his hardened piece, and I remember slithering across the carpet toward the balcony doors for no particular reason, propelled by a thrusting cock and searching hands. He was laughing and telling me how nice and tight my ass was. I was almost to the glass doors and could see the waves crashing against the Honolulu hotel coast beach, with a full moon shimmering above, when he unloaded his first spouting of cream inside me.

With almost no rest from that, he hauled me up to the foot of the bed and laid me down there, on my side, my right hip on the end of the bed, my left leg bent up at the knee on the bed, and my right one suspended awkwardly out beyond the bed. He was covering me with his lean, sinewy body and was kissing my lips and nipples and burying his nose and tongue in my armpits. He lifted my left leg with a hand then and skewered me again with a long, but not particularly thick cock. His cock head kissed the walls of my ass canal as he plowed up into me, and I moaned at this second, quick-thrusting fucking. He stroked me endlessly this time, turning me this way and that way, making full use of his extraordinary flexibility, and giving every square inch of my ass canal walls and the rim and prostate caressing attention. I came this time, stroking myself as he was stroking inside me—and he came as well in a second great profusion of semen. I had never thought of English men being this virile, vigorous, and full of jism.

He held me there on the bed, panting and exhausted, for I don't know how long. But there was a band of purple and orange at the horizon off the Honolulu beach when he half guided and half carried me out onto the balcony and lowered me into a chaise lounge. He set me down on the small of my back, with a pillow behind me for support and lifted my legs and spread them wide on top of the short arms of the chaise. Then, straddling the bed of the chaise with his strong, muscled legs, facing me, he held and jerked our cocks together until they were both hard again and then he lifted my buttocks with the long, elegant fingers of his strong hands and moved his pelvis into mine, running his long cock up into me again in a long, gliding motion. I threw my head back and held my breath as his cock snaked up my canal and let my breath out in a cry of welcome and ecstasy as his reddish pubic hairs nestled against my tender butt cheeks. He held there for the longest time, bringing his mouth to mine for a deep kiss, and then he stroked in and out of me, climaxing to his third prodigious ejaculation of the night, while I watched the sun rise over the Pacific over the bobbing head that was sucking so delightedly on my nipples.

The Director must have been pleased with my performance that night in his hotel suite, because I moved in with him the next day for the rest of the program shoot. Then over the next couple of years, while I was living in Washington, D.C., he had me come out to L.A. for work a few other popular American detective and amateur sleuth program series. I was established by then as an editor, including screen editing, so I wasn't always in front of the cameras. Sometimes when I was on the set I'd be roomed with him for some hot nights of vigorous fucking and sometimes he just had me to his trailer for nooners—and sometimes both. He made full use of his gymnastic past in our sessions on his dressing room couch, taking me repeatedly in some of the most inventive and hot positions I'd known before or experienced since.

We drifted apart when I was once more assigned to Thailand and no longer could fly into L.A. on short notice for work as an extra or script editor, but he helped make my "sometimes" film career memorable, exhausting, and a butt aching.

Chapter Fourteen: That One Exception

I have always managed to keep my bi world in check and separate from my public straight world by always putting my wife and children first and by committing only to them—that is, possibly, with one notable exception. I had an atypical long-term relationship with an Australian colleague that seemed innocuous at least at the beginning but that has grown stronger over the years—possibly beyond the grave.

I briefly knew Ian during a temporary assignment in Okinawa, Japan, where we were coworkers. He was one of those very intelligent, happy-go-lucky Aussies of ruddy complexion, a slightly stocky build, and a kind and friendly word for everyone. He seemed a surface kind of guy who did his work with competence, didn't muck around in office politics, and headed straight for the sports bar and an evening of beer and witty banter at the end of his shift. I was new to the office, and he had quickly become an old hand at all of the procedures. I gravitated toward him immediately as the most knowledgeable and "head straight from here to there" worker on board.

I probably wouldn't have gotten to know Ian beyond superficial office interaction during this time, however, if I wasn't starved for practice tennis partners to keep my skills from atrophying. He didn't look the part of a competitive sportsman, and he was quite clear that he didn't really play much tennis, rather that he played handball and squash. But when we got on the tennis court, I quickly learned that squash players had some wicked moves that served them in good stead in tennis. He would run me ragged on the court and by the time I left my temporary duty, he was regularly beating me—and I was quite a competent player.

Ian was as humble in his quick mastery of this sport that was new to him as he was in everything else he did. He never was arrogant about his abilities and always was in the background at work, helping all and letting them take full credit, even though he probably was the smartest and most competent person in the room. I considered him a comfortable, nonthreatening, casual buddy. We showered together at the club after vigorous tennis sessions. And it was after these sessions that we started to become close. We'd sit out on the deck at the club bar and enjoy a couple of beers together and we chatted—and our chats led to ever-deeper conversations about world events that our job brought close to us and about our families and ourselves.

He was divorced from an early, and very short-lived marriage, and I was married, but in an open marriage in which my wife and I, working for the same government agency, often found ourselves apart and in different parts of the world for long periods of time.

I returned to the States in preparation for a job in Bangkok and he was reassigned to the same Bangkok office I would join. Once again, he already knew the ropes at work before I arrived and, once again, he became both a mentor and a tennis practice partner for me, even though I far outranked him in the office. These were days when I was awakening to the bi lifestyle and becoming very active with men, and my relationship with Ian, although well separated from my bi world, developed to the point that I didn't keep that sexual awakening and blossoming of mine from him. My trust in his discretion was total.

And then one day Ian just resigned his position and walked away from his job. He moved to Hong Kong and became a correspondent for a major international news agency.

I visited with him once in Hong Kong when I was passing through there, but he seemed a little strained and distant. We corresponded sporadically for a year, but he suddenly stopped answering my letters.

I sometimes thought of him with a mild sense of regret that we had lost touch.

A couple of years after that I was sent to an international conference in Tokyo as part of the American delegation. To my surprise, I saw that Ian was there as well, covering the conference for his news agency. We could hardly avoid seeing each other, and after a somewhat awkward moment of mutual recognition and terse exchanges of essential "since we last met" information, we arranged to go to lunch the following day.

Lunch at the coffee shop in the Okura Hotel, the venue of the conference, went well, and almost instantaneously we were back to our chatty selves of the Bangkok and Okinawa years. I didn't hold back on my continued bi activity in Bangkok, something that I shared with almost no one, and Ian didn't make any disparaging comment on that. At the end of the lunch, he asked me if I would meet him after the conference session had ended that day and take a walk with him. I readily agreed, suddenly hungry for contact with the friend who had drifted away from me.

We took the subway to the Shinjuku Gyoen National Garden, the many-acre grounds of a former palace in the heart of the city. And we walked and we talked and we lost all track of time.

Ian asked me if I'd go to a bar in a nearby Shinjuku district with him for a drink, and, of course, I was pleased to do so, anxious to prolong the comfortable contact that I was beginning to realize I had long missed.

I was somewhat nonplussed, though, when he led me into the Shinjuku Ni-chome area, the main gay district of Tokyo. I wasn't at all sure that Ian realized where we were, but he headed straight for a particular club that he must have picked out beforehand. It was a performance nightclub, and the host led us to a banquette very near the stage. I sat there in awkward silence next to Ian, as a slight Japanese youth got fucked by a big-cocked northern European on stage, just a few steps from our table.

"Ian," I said in a low voice. "What is this? Are you trying to tell me something?"

"I can't hold this in any longer," Ian replied. "I think I must bring this out in the open at a place like this."

"Ian," I continued. "Are you trying to tell me you are gay? If so, for how long have you kept this from me? And why did you break off contact—because I've just realized that this is what you did. You broke off contact with me."

"No, I'm not gay—at least in the sense of having done it with a man," Ian said, a very serious and intense look on his face. "But when we were working together and getting to know each other, and you were so open with me on what you were doing with other men, I grew to want you myself. And you never looked my way. I could never tell you, and I couldn't even work out at the time what I wanted from you. But in the end I just snapped."

"And that was why you quit in Bangkok and took this job?" I asked. "Because of me?"

"Yes," Ian answered. "Because I couldn't stand being around you any longer without being part of your world. And yet I was scared to become part of your world. I didn't even know if I could be part of your world."

"And that's why you stood off when I visited you in Hong Kong and why you stopped answering my letters?" I asked.

"Yes, yes, I guess so. It wasn't intentional really; I just couldn't bring myself to continue pursuing what seemed to be the impossible. I couldn't take the frustration. It was all just too painful."

"And now?" I asked.

"Now that I've seen you again, I don't think I can go on without being part of your world. But you probably have no interest in someone like me. I just don't know how to move in any direction from here. I just know that bringing you here was the most direct statement I could make of what I wanted and what I was prepared to do to arrive at that place."

We went silent then, and we both watched the small Japanese youth being stuffed vigorously by the huge European. The youth was cuffed at all four points on a x-shaped metal apparatus, the upper part shorter than the lower and crossing at the young man's sternum. His bondage spread his arms and legs in a standing position and gave the European open access to both his ass and cock and balls. The European was pounding the former with his own cock and worrying the latter with his gripping hands. It sounded like some of the young Japanese fellow's screams of ecstasy at least were genuine and that it wasn't all an act.

I watched Ian watching the performance. He didn't seem repelled by it, but he didn't seem overly aroused by it either. I thought long and hard about our situation, but what was coming to the surface were those feelings of loss that periodically had pierced me. It dawned on me that I valued my once-lost relationship with Ian very much. Perhaps much more than with almost anyone else; that I had been intimate with men I regarded and wanted to be with far less than I was finding I wanted to be with Ian.

I put my hand on top of Ian's. "Whose hotel is closest, Ian?"

Ian gave me an intense look, and I could see that he was struggling for what to say. At length he just whispered in a husky voice, "I'm all the way out near Narita airport. You?"

"I'm just over on Roppongi. At the New Japan. Just about a fifteen-minute walk."

We stared at each other, no longer watching the performance, although a second man, togged out skimpily in leathers, had arrived to join in tormenting the Japanese captive for our viewing pleasure.

"Are you sure, Ian?" I asked, trying to give him every opportunity to back out. "I can do this. I feel closer to you than to any other man I know. I realize that now. But are you sure this is for you?"

"With you, yes," he simply stated. "Having seen you again, I can no longer think of life without you."

I took him back to my room at the New Japan, which was one of those then-new idea hotels where the rooms were very small and all of the furniture was one molded continuous unit of bed, dresser, night stand, and attached lounge chair. The decor was a flamboyant red, white, and gold, and the bed stood out so prominently that there was no question what the main focal point was.

"Can you undress for me?" Ian asked meekly after he had sat down in the only chair. "I've only gotten furtive looks at you in the shower when we were playing tennis. But I want to see you."

I complied, and when I had stripped I stood there for him.

"Wow," was all he could say at first.

I said nothing. It was not the least immodest or unrealistic for me to know that we were worlds apart in surface sex appeal, and I didn't want him to have second thoughts and to flee the room.

But then, after a few moments, he continued on his own. "Can I touch you? Can I see what it's like to take you in my mouth."

I came over and stood in front of him as he sat in the chair unit, very close, and I held his head in my hands patiently, tenderly as he clumsily kissed and tongued and sucked my cock. It was the worst blow job I'd ever had. It was the best, most loving blow job I'd ever had. I barely could contain my tears at what Ian was giving me—and what it was costing him to do so.

Before I could climax, I gently reached down and pulled him up and slowly took his clothes off. When he was naked, I turned and laid him down on the bed. He was extremely self-conscious and kept trying to cover his manhood with his hands and shrink his body into invisibility.

"I'm sorry," he stammered. "I know I'm not what you're used to . . ."

"Shush," I whispered in a stroking voice. "You are beautiful to me. And you are all mine. Don't cover yourself from me. Open to me. Spread your legs to me. Welcome me and let me possess you fully. Give yourself to me."

Showing how much he wanted this and his trust in me, he moved his hands to above his head on the bed, stretching his slightly paunchy torso out, and spread his legs for me.

I lovingly prepared his virgin ass with my lips and tongue and with lubricant I pulled from the nightstand drawer. I ran one of his well-muscled legs up my torso and held the other one out from his body with a hand wrapped around his ankle. I was as gentle as I could be when I started working my cock into his ass. I could tell that he wanted to scream, however, but was determined not to. I turned and opened the nightstand drawer again and found, appropriately, a thick padded headband I used to keep the sweat out of my eyes when I played tennis. I told him to open his mouth, and I pushed this between his teeth to give him something to help him bite through the pain and not to scream. I knew that it was important to him that he not scream at his loss of innocence.

I pumped him very slowly as his ass became accustomed to the invading cock. It wasn't all that long before he quieted down and the pleasure was pushing out his pain. He began undulating under me, telling me what a strange and new and filling feeling this was—and how close this made him feel to me and how wonderful I was and how sexy I made him feel. He was babbling now, learning what being intimate with me entailed, and discovering he could handle it—that he loved it—that he would feel us learning to move as one in a magnificent, close coupling.

Overwhelmed by this new activity, he shot his load up his belly a long time before I climaxed inside him. When I was done, I started to turn to go into the bathroom and clean myself off. But Ian pulled me down to him and our limbs became entwined as rolled around on the narrow bed, fighting to get closer to each other, to dissolve into one body. Exhausted finally, we lay there all akimbo and connected, the sheets twisted around and between us. We moved immediately then into our old bantering pillow talk of our lives and likes and of world affairs and our own involvement in that—almost as if we had done the same thing the day before. But now we were on my hotel bed and in each other's arms, our hands exploring each other, making sure that the other was real, was still there.

When we momentarily ran out of talk, we began kissing and caressing each other's bodies again, and I fucked Ian a second time in a languid side split. We slept then—nearly the whole night—and I was awakened with Ian's whispered request that I possess him again. And I did, turning him on his belly and covering his body with mine and pushing my cock into his ass to the hilt and rotating my cock around inside him, searching for every nock and cranny. Leaving my mark everywhere inside him to stake my claim that he was mine fully, and no one else's.

Shortly after I returned to Bangkok from the conference, Ian managed to be rehired by my agency and, surprise, surprise, be assigned to the Bangkok office. My wife and family were in country now, and Ian met and married a fine, intelligent and gentle Southeast Asian woman who worked for us. But we still managed to meet frequently for tennis and discussion and a languid fuck in small Bangkok hour-rate hotels specializing in such assignations.

When my tour of duty in Bangkok was over, I returned to the States and received other foreign assignments. Ian left my agency's employ yet again and returned to his foreign correspondent job. Over the years and across the world, we managed to schedule long weekends together, where we would share sightseeing, good food, great wine, long talks, and gentle lovemaking.

Ian, who was a few years younger than I was, moved back to Australia with his wife and children and prepared for an early retirement. I now was permanently settled back in the United States. We were arranging a long weekend together in London when I received word he had died suddenly of a heart attack. That was two years ago, but I still think of him and have an empty spot in my heart with "Ian" written indelibly across it. He has left his mark of full possession inside me as well. It matters not that he's no longer here in the flesh. It isn't always about flesh.

Chapter Fifteen: Rude Awakening

The most wonderful thing a lover has ever done for me was to give me my life. I didn't understand it at the time, but if he had loved me as I wanted him to—as I begged him to—I would be long dead today.

The days of my sexual coming of age in Bangkok, Thailand, during the early mid seventies through the mid eighties were paradise followed by a rude awakening, a realization of how life can come back at you hard that I didn't fully realize until I had left the City of the Angels. Bangkok was an open city with no sense of moral wrong. If you could afford it and enjoyed it, more power to you, and no one would pass judgment, let alone hassle you. It was the tail end of the "free love" hippy era, before the realization of the existence of AIDS or the widespread use of condoms. It was flesh on and in flesh and do whatever jacks you off.

I ached for Daren, who, along with the hairdresser lover he had finagled into the country with a diplomatic passport, lived in the same apartment compound I did. Daren was a U.S. diplomat, who made flights every other week in and out of Saigon to register and transport the bastard children of U.S. servicemen from the recent war who the Hanoi regime was permitting to leave the country for a high price.

Daren was a magnificent black man, solidly built and beautiful in every way. His lover had come over officially as the tutor of Daren's three children, but the children had returned to their mother in the States within two months and the hairdresser stayed on and became the darling of the international set. Daren's wife was obviously one of the most understanding of human beings, but she never visited Bangkok while Daren was there as far as I knew.

The hairdresser, Jamie, was also nice to look at; a lithe blond, cute but submissive, with fluid moves and bent wrists. But it was Daren who I had my eyes on. I did everything I could to get myself close to Daren and to make him understand that he could have me any way he wanted me. And he was very friendly to me and slowly let me enter his circle of friends, mostly local Thai gay boys, who didn't attract me all that much. But he didn't even touch me for the longest time.

I knew he could give good sex, because I walked in on him and the hairdresser doing the hot and heavy in their apartment one day and stayed around to watch. It was an inspiring and deeply sensual performance of coffee and cream. Both were naked. Daren was as beautiful in the nude as I could have imagined him to be in my wildest dreams. His cock was long and hard and thick, and when I walked in, he was slowly stroking it in and out of Jamie's ass in a languid, fluid motion. Jamie's back was flat on the bed, and Daren was standing below him and arched over his body. One of Jamie's legs ran up Daren's torso and Daren was holding the other one up and out. Daren was running his free hand over Jamie's chest, belly, thighs, cock, and balls. Occasionally he would take the root of his own cock in his hand and rotate it in Jamie's ass at great depth. Jamie would arch his back and rotate his hips in rhythm with Daren's moves and sigh and moan. I could tell that Daren was fully satisfying him. And I wanted Daren to fully satisfy me, as well—and, maybe, instead of Jamie, if the truth be known.

Right before Daren ejaculated inside Jamie; he brought his lips down to the hollow of Jamie's neck and kissed him deeply there. Jamie turned his face toward me. His eyes were droopy and hooded; he looked like they were swimming in Daren's semen, and I hated him for that. He gave me a satisfied "I've got what you want" smile and then Daren turned his head and they went into a long kiss, during which Jamie continued to writhe in pleasure until his body jerked and he shot cum up onto Daren's belly. I turned and left the room in frustration and jealously.

I did eventually have sex with Daren, but it was nothing like the sex he had with Jamie. On several occasions we got into heavy petting on his pillow-strewn sofa, always when Jamie was off doing someone's hair. Daren would never touch me when Jamie was there.

Our first sexual encounter was in the southern peninsula district of Thailand where we had gone on an American embassy cultural program. Daren had a magnificent baritone singing voice, and as I had been a professional tenor, we had been teamed up to give cultural exchange concerts around Southeast Asia. The hotel we were staying at was a small one on the beach across from some peculiar—and spectacular—outcroppings that arose from the sea just off the coast and that had figured in one of the then-recent James Bond films. The hotel was so small that Daren and I had to share a room. The setting was exotic and the twilight was so romantic that we found ourselves in each other's arms on a lounge chair we had found on the balcony outside our room. I atypically was the aggressor. I tried to kiss Daren on the lips, but he avoided that. He however allowed me to kiss his nipples and all around his torso until my lips dipped lower than his navel. He then brought my head back up to his chest and murmured that we could stroke each other off but no cocksucking, fucking, or even kissing on the lips.

I was extremely disappointed and angry at the hold that Jamie seemed to have on Daren, but I did come quickly to the magic touch of his hands stroking my cock, and he sighed and moaned satisfactorily at my own hand job on his dick.

On the occasions when Daren and I subsequently sex, we would undress each other—which didn't take much effort as there never was much being worn in the tropics anyway. As in our initial coupling, he never let me kiss him on the lips or on the cock or asshole, and he wouldn't do that for me either, but kisses elsewhere and "feels" anywhere were permitted. Our cuddlings and pettings usually ended with Daren straddling me from behind, his cock dry fucking up from the small of my back, and him running his hands over my chest and belly and thighs and stroking my cock until I came. He'd have his face buried in the hollow of my neck from behind, and when he jacked off up my back, he would murmur how nice my body was and how much he'd enjoyed our lovemaking as he carefully wiped his cum off my back. It didn't sound like much, but Daren was so beautiful that I think I could have come just by us sitting there and looking at each other.

I had convinced myself that Daren had such a loyalty to Jamie that he would only be that intimate with one lover, and I fought with myself for months to respect that loyalty. But I was thoroughly confused and angered one day when I walked in to find him pumping his Thai houseboy from behind across the back of a chair, with both of them screaming with joy as Daren came. The houseboy had immediately turned and kneeled and cleaned Daren's cock with his tongue. And Daren had let him do this and obviously had enjoyed it—so much for the loyalty theory.

The next day when Jamie left to puff up some ambassador's wife's beehive, I stormed into Daren's apartment and tried to force myself on him, to make him fuck me like he fucked Jamie. But Daren, considerably stronger than I was, pushed me to the door as gently as he could and, voicing his regrets that we needed to stop seeing each other, locked it behind me.

From that day forward, Daren's door was closed and locked to me. And I hadn't gotten over the frustration and anger on the day I left Bangkok for my next assignment.

Within a year both Daren and Jamie—and presumably the Thai houseboy and most of Daren's Thai gay crowd—were dead. They had contracted AIDS, something I knew nothing about until long after I had left Bangkok, something that no one openly acknowledged was stalking the gay community in Bangkok while I was there. I had loved freely and frequently while I was in

Bangkok, and it was a miracle that I never contracted AIDS myself. But Daren had made sure that I wouldn't contract it from him. After he learned of the disease and that he had it and had received a death sentence, he very carefully never again exchanged body fluids with anyone he didn't know was as infected already as he was.

No lover before or since has given me what Daren did. He gave me my life.

Chapter Sixteen: Cockpitting

After two years in the male-male paradise of Bangkok, a short assignment to Okinawa, Japan, seemed, for most of my tour, like entering a monastery. I was supposed to rotate directly back to the States with my SR71 supersonic photoreconnaissance unit, but the North Koreans were acting up on the DMZ, and the government wanted an intense look-see at whether or not they were building their troop strength up near the border. The flying from Kadena Airbase was fine, but, as far as sexual release, Okinawa seemed pretty much a wasteland compared to Bangkok.

Neither the local women nor men were all that attractive in general and they were wholly unsophisticated and unimaginative in terms of pursuing the options for self-satisfaction. There were some luscious soldiers, airmen, and sailors about, but the U.S. authorities kept them on a pretty short leash, and I wasn't going to be on "the Rock" long enough to develop many liaisons.

If it hadn't been for Keith, another photorecon jet driver on temporary assignment from Bangkok, I definitely would have felt sexually deprived. We had been in the same group of "fuck buddies" back in Bangkok, and we managed to get on the same shift rotation at Kadena. Pilots were put on call for twenty-four-hour shifts, which meant that when we were on duty rotation, we ate and slept in a Quonset hut attached to the hangar housing our two Blackbirds, just waiting for the call to leap into the air and shoot pictures of suspected North Korean troop movements.

A couple of times a week Keith and I would find ourselves alone in the Quonset bunk room, and, on these occasions, we never needed more than one bunk.

One night Keith had me on my back, sidewise on the bottom bunk, with my feet lodged wide apart in the railings undergirding the upper bunk and my hands hanging on to the tailings of the sheets and covers of the upper bunk, while Keith stood on the floor next to the bunk, hunched down, and with his cock pounding away at my chute. He was a real moaner and must have been enjoying his plowing of my ass immensely that night, because we attracted the attention of an airman doing some late-night maintenance on the SR71s.

The airman was a big muscular blond, and he had a grin that went from ear to ear as he draped himself in the Quonset hut doorway and watched Keith fuck me. He wasn't the type who was satisfied with just watching, though, and in short order he had saddled up behind Keith, and the heightening of the decibel rate of Keith's moans let me know that he was being plowed from behind while he was mining my ass.

The airman must have taken a particular fancy to me, because as Keith was finishing, the airman had pushed his head over Keith's shoulder and was in a lip lock with me.

He hadn't come when Keith shot off and collapsed beside me on the bed in a panting heap, and he disengaged from Keith at that point and sat down on the other side of me and continued kissing me and pulling at his engorged rod.

"I wanna do you," he was whispering to me.

"So, who's stopping you?" I asked. I liked repeated fuckings by multiple men.

"Not here." he whispered back to me.

"Where then?" was my reply.

"In the bird, man. In the cockpit of the bird."

I was skeptical as to whether we really could do it in the cockpit of the SR71, but we managed. It was a tight fit—in more ways than one. There is very little room for my thighs beside his on the seat as he sat in the driver's seat and I faced him and lowered my ass on his rod. In addition to that, his dick was so thick that this was a tight fit in my ass as well.

I pole danced for a short while, sliding up and down his pole, but then he took control. He lifted my legs up around and behind him onto the cowling of the plane behind the cockpit, with me leaning my back against the instrument panel, and he rode my ass hard in deep upward thrusts that had the jet rocking back and forth on its wheels.

This was every bit as good a fuck as I had been getting in Bangkok.

I learned that my well-hung and horny airman technician's name was Pete. I didn't learn this because he said anything to me that night. He, in fact, left me bent over the cowling behind the cockpit of the SR71 and gasping for air that night, never having identified himself.

But he apparently knew my name, as I was to learn later.

I was fascinated with the medieval castles that could be found in ruins on the small Pacific island. Okinawa had long been real estate that both China and Japan had contended for and, in turn, had forcibly occupied. But the castles of Okinawa were eerily similar to those of medieval Western Europe even though those two cultures apparently never made contact. Before I left the island on my short tour there, I wanted to explore those castles, and the opportunity arose when the Kadena AFB Outing Club posted a tour of one of the best-preserved castles near Bolo Point, on the island's west coast, nearly at the halfway point from north to south.

I didn't think anything of it when the tour leader called me to tell me there needed to be a change in the tour date. I didn't even think twice when he went out of his way to ensure that I could go on the tour on the new date and time.

On the appointed day, I appeared at the recreation building in the Quonset hut near the Koza City Gate Number Two to the air base.

That's when I got my surprise. The tour guide was Pete, the guy who had flown me a couple of weeks earlier in the cockpit of the SR71. He was even hunkier in the daylight than he had been in the airplane hangar late at night.

He introduced himself to me quite politely, acting like he hadn't known me already in the biblical sense, and told me it would be just the two of us riding out to Bolo Point in his jeep—that the rest of the hikers would meet us at the castle.

It was a good thing we took the jeep, because the castle was on top of a craggy outcropping accessible only by a narrow track through a sugarcane field. There weren't any other vehicles on the small cleared apron in front of the castle gate when we arrived; nor were there any other tour takers in evidence—or anyone else for that matter. This was really a remote spot of the island.

When we entered the shadows of the small enclosure between the outer and inner gates, Pete pushed me up against a crumbling, gray stone wall and placed strong hands on the wall on either side of me.

"I have a confession to make," he told me in a low, husky voice.

"Oh?" was all I could manage. I was breathless with anticipation. That night in the jet cockpit had been the best sex I'd had during my Okinawa tour. I was his for the asking.

"The tour wasn't really rescheduled. I saw your name on the roster, and I wanted to give you a private tour," he said, brushing his hand against the side of my face. "Do you mind?"

"No, not at all," I answered in a hoarse voice.

"May I kiss you?" He asked

I assented with a nod and by turning my head to him, and he kissed me deeply and tenderly.

"I haven't thought of anything but you since that night," he said when we'd come up for air. "May I fuck you again?"

My answer was a foregone conclusion. I'd already acknowledged to myself that I was his for the asking, and he'd asked me politely, which hadn't always been the case with my lusty partners. I did, however, make him give me at least a perfunctory tour of the castle first, as my interest in that was genuine, as was the expertise of his tour guiding.

What was most striking in the comparison of Western castles and those of ancient Okinawa was the fundamental difference in their plans. The stonework, towers, and battlements were all quite similar, but whereas a Western castle tended to be fortified from the edges in, with the most precious holdings located at the center, the Okinawan castle invariably was built against a precipice, as this one was, with the holy of holies being a sacred grove and ruling family altar at the rear of the castle, hanging on at the top of the cliff.

After a brief tour of the outer works of the castle, Pete guided me back to the sacred grove, which was just that, a grove of pine trees at the very back of the castle walls on a small apron of land suspended over the boiling surf at the foot of the cliff. Here there was a grassy area in the middle of the grove of trees and a stone altar—the center of the ancestor worship for the family that once had ruled the castle and the surrounding fields and had acted as the sentinel for invasion from China to the west or the Japanese islands to the north.

Pete laid out a khaki army blanket on the ground in front of the altar, and after pulling me to him in a standing position and fondling and kissing me into a lustful mood, he undressed me, pushed me down on all fours, prepared my asshole with his tongue and saliva, and covered with his body and fucked me to paradise. As he pumped me, I listened to the roaring surf at the base of the cliff and the wind sighing in the pine trees, and I added my own sighs and moans of ecstasy to the sounds of nature.

When we both had come, Pete pulled me over on my side within his arms and we both merged with the wild beauty of the setting until our breathing had regularized. We then kissed and worked each other's bodies with our hands until we were in full rut once more.

Pete pulled me up from the ground and took the army blanket and draped it over the stone altar in the middle of the grove. He then pushed me onto my back on top of the altar, spread my legs wide, and we worshipped the exuberance of our youth and vitality and our healthy, lustful bodies at the altar with merging and rhythmic thrusts and counterthrusts and with me crying my passion to the tops of the swaying pine trees.

In Pete I at last found my escape from the somewhat tedious routine of the Okinawa assignment, but I had hardly found him and started to be introduced to a very active male-male underculture on the island, when my government decided that the North Koreans were just rattling rockets they didn't actually have, and I was on my way east across the Pacific Ocean, leaving Pete and the fascinating Okinawan castles behind.

Chapter Seventeen: The Ethiopian Cabin Boy

When I left Bangkok, Thailand, the first time, I originally thought I'd be returning to a world that was almost completely straight and that my days of enjoying a rich and active bi lifestyle were over. My work with the government, with its strong homophobic policies, just didn't seem to leave that avenue safely open to me. And for a couple of years, when I was assigned to Washington, D.C., and was retraining to work on the ground to unravel secrets for the United States as I had recently been doing high overhead as a photoreconnaissance jet driver, my sex life was pretty heterosexual.

But to my surprise, when I was training for intelligence gathering, I discovered that my line of work wasn't as pristine sexually as I had tried to convince myself it was. I should already have been aware of this, as I had already gotten more than hints—personal experience, in fact—of my spy masters looking the other direction in Bangkok when it pleased them to do so. And in my training, I learned that they could be pleased to do so if the intelligence needed was considered very important and when the options of "getting the goods" were restricted.

I was sent into the Middle East and stationed in Cyprus, which is now considered in relationship to the Middle East somewhat like Switzerland was considered to Europe in World War II—a safe haven where spies can meet on neutral ground and where it is considered ungentlemanly (although it does happen on occasion) for "wet" (meaning doing someone to death) operations to be conducted. And it wasn't long before I learned how far I might be expected to go to "get the goods" in my job. It was also where I quickly found a new answer to one of three questions that had perpetually come up in the world of "bottoms" in my Bangkok days: This question was "What was your longest?" One of the other questions, "What was your thickest?" would also be answered when I lived on Cyprus, but during a different tour a decade later. The remaining question, "What was the most satisfying?" had had already been answered years earlier in Bangkok in the form of a black Army officer (who, with his celebrated ten by two dimensions, almost answered the other two questions as well).

The "longest" question was answered in the form of an Ethiopian cabin boy on the yacht of a Saudi businessman at anchor off the Larnaka waterfront. This promenade, very European in atmosphere, enjoys a deep, flat beach separated from a long hotel and sidewalk café front of gaily decorated umbrellas and tables by a wide boulevard. The boulevard is anchored at one end by a yacht marina and at the other by the medieval harbor castle where Richard the Lionhearted married his shipwrecked Berengaria.

After our encounter, the Ethiopian had me singing a couple of octaves higher than normal and walking around tenderly—although the later part might have been caused by the escapades later that night. I can't attest to how long the Ethiopian's cock was, but both my eyes and my intestines are quite sure they've never seen or felt a longer one.

When he took me, we were in a lower-deck cabin of the yacht, where you couldn't stand up straight except in the middle of the cabin. A double bed went in under the bulkhead. The Saudi owner of the yacht and I had just agreed on some successful business of a nefarious government nature, and the Saudi had been very attentive to me and let me know he wanted to fuck me.

I had met him at a couple of embassy cocktail parties earlier and apparently had made a very favorable impression on him. I could tell by the way he looked at me that he fancied me, but I didn't make the connection at the time when I was assigned to contact him.

My spy masters wanted the deal to go well, and I had been told to do what it took to conclude the deal—and I subsequently came to assume that my masters knew exactly what the Saudi businessman was interested in getting in return for his vital information—that they had assigned me to this task precisely because the Saudi fancied me. So, when he so directly propositioned me and connected it with his willingness to provide what I had come for, I said I would sleep with him that night on the yacht. Clearly delighted, he responded that, in appreciation, he'd send me a gift before dinner.

An Ethiopian cabin boy—not a "boy," of course, but a young man—had been gliding around the yacht all day, doing this and that, as the vessel wallowed off the colorful Larnaka waterfront. He was incredibly tall and thin, really out of place on a yacht with cramped head room, even if it was large. When I opened the door of my cabin to him, he was carrying a tray with a bottle of champagne and one glass on it, but I knew right away that he was my gift, because he was nude. His pecker hung down almost to his knees, it seemed—and his thighs were unusually long in themselves. I had never really thought about whether the unusual height on some African tribesmen had a relationship to dimensions elsewhere, but just then my education in that department lengthened considerably.

There was no thought of me refusing this gift from the Saudi; he hadn't given me the promised information yet, and this was no time to rock the boat—other than the rocking the Ethiopian was about to do with his performance on my body, of course.

I was still in just my Speedo, so there wasn't much undressing required. The tray also had a bottle of KY and a couple of condom packets on it, and the Ethiopian just slid off my Speedo and knelt there and sucked me hard, while pulling his own meat to erection. I fell back onto the bed, which was low to the floor, while he lathered himself and my hole up. He wishboned my legs up and out and I dug my feet into the low bulkhead that stretched out over the bed. He then knelt between my legs and just fed and fed and fed and fed that long eleven- or twelve-incher up into me.

At first he moved my hand to my ass and had me cup my fingers there so that he was pushing his cock through my cupped fingers, giving him a hand job as well as him giving me an ass fuck, when he entered me. Before I was able to open entirely up to him, there was as much length of his cock outside of my channel as most men can boast in total. I gasped as he reached a depth inside me I'd rarely felt before even though he had to go several inches through my fingers before entering me. But he laughed hoarsely as I panted and moaned to accommodate him. And then he brushed my hand away and I arched my back and cried out my astonishment and passion as he just dug deeper and deeper inside me. It wasn't all that painful, because his cock was pretty thin, but he had to have gotten well up into my intestines and stretched them out where they'd never been touched from that direction by a foreign object before, colonoscopies being something in my far future still.

I looked up as he was doing this, and the Saudi was lounging in the doorway watching me get royally fucked. The Ethiopian pumped me that way for a while and then turned me over on my belly and got that cock even farther up into me, taking it all out and then just slamming all the way back in repeatedly until he needed to come. And he withdrew, jerked off his condom, and shot off all over the small of my back. I was digging my fists into the bedding as best I could to hold position while he jackhammered into me. I'd already come twice by then myself, once with the help of his mouth and then with the help of his hand.

The Saudi just stood there and watched with slitted eyes. He kept his hand busy with his own cock. His "gift" to me was even more another gift to himself. He really wanted his entertainment worth for those precious secrets he held, and the long, long Ethiopian and I gave him quite a show.

That night the Saudi and his bulky bodyguard did me in a sandwich in an all-night fuck fest in the main cabin, which was not nearly as cramped as mine was. The Saudi's equipment was nothing to write home about and he came quickly, but the bodyguard had a really thick piece and was a fast reloader and had a vigorous, long-endurance pelvis action. Lots of nice muscle. He's probably the one who was responsible for my bowed legs and shuffling walk—and big smile—the next day.

They did me in turn. Then, as a finale, the Saudi really wanted to get his cock in there with the bodyguard's, but I wasn't having any of that, needed secrets or not. The bodyguard alone was much too thick.

I never did drink the champagne, and I can only surmise that the information I collected was worth my effort—at least my masters were well pleased when I returned, and they asked me no questions about my use of trade craft in getting the goods.

Chapter Eighteen: Norwegian Stallion

One of the saddest—and most ironic—casualties of the internecine Greek-Turkish war on Cyprus that divided the island into warring camps four decades ago was the once-famous and elegant Ledra Palace Hotel. The Treaty Room of the Ledra Palace, a hulking stone edifice in the Moorish style, had been the venue where the British secretly committed the crime of slicing up the Arabian Peninsula and Levant at the end of World War I in a purposeful—and highly successful—effort to make political boundaries perpetually volatile there. A similar travesty was to be committed in the same room by the same British in the early 1970s, when, with a green grease pencil, a British officer drew the "Green Line" cease-fire boundary separating Greek Cypriots from Turkish Cypriots. The irony for the hotel, was that this green line went right through the hotel itself, indeed down the center of the Treaty Room, condemning the once five-star hotel to the oblivion of a no man's land. The building subsequently was taken over by the United Nations peacekeeping contingent as a barracks for its troops.

This all led, in a roundabout way, to my memories of the most exuberant and playful lover I've ever had—not to mention the thickest cock I've ever taken.

Foreign diplomats like me in Cyprus were permitted to cross between the Greek Cypriot and Turkish Cypriot zones, but there was only one always-available border crossing, and that was on the street running right by the entrance to the Ledra Palace Hotel in the center of the capital city, Nicosia.

Our cars had to stop at, first, the Greek checkpoint right under the front balconies of the Ledra Palace, and then drive slowly through the UN-controlled buffer zone and stop again for a document check at the Turkish checkpoint.

I credit the military unit sign above the entrance to the hotel, now UN barracks, for my becoming Svend's man toy. I had stepped out of my car while the soldiers at the Greek checkpoint were checking my diplomatic passport, and I looked up and smiled at the new unit sign, which said "The Norwegian Stallions." I found that so incongruous, expecting "stallions" to be used for a military unit from the American West and for Scandinavians to use something like "Vikings," instead, and this incongruity made me smile broadly.

At first I didn't see Svend, sitting on a stone balcony just above and to the left of the unit sign. If I had seen him first, the "stallion" name wouldn't have seemed incongruous to me, and we probably never would have met. He was a magnificent blond hulk, and he was sitting wearing only a pair of loose khaki shorts in a rickety chair braced back against the wall. When my eyes did turn to him, seeking a slight movement at the periphery of my vision, the smile was still plastered on my face. His shorts were so loose at the legs that, with his propped back position, I could see all the way up his legs to a thick cock and a pair of huge balls. He stared cockily down at me, obviously very pleased with himself—and fully knowing his manhood was exposed to me—and with every right to be pleased with himself. He was one hung male stud in his full glory.

I do remember having a fleeting impression of him smiling broadly back at me, but just then the Greeks were finished trying, as their usual wont, albeit halfheartedly, to dissuade me from driving into the Turkish enemy's camp, and I was on my way.

The whole incident didn't really make that much of an impression on me—or so I thought. I was crossing the border on an important mission. If I hadn't been preoccupied with that, that Norwegian beauty probably would have haunted me for some time thereafter. But weeks later, when I found myself temporarily alone in Nicosia without family, I took advantage of sneaking into an underground gay bar in the suburb of Makedonitissa, very near to the main UN base inside the buffer zone.

I was at the bar, quietly drinking—a bit too much, I'm afraid—and taking in the gay scene around me, when a Norse god saddled up beside me. He looked sort of familiar, but not really. But he certainly looked good—all muscle and square-jawed good looks.

"Hello again, my name is Svend."

"Hello," I answered. "But again? Do I know you?" I had kept my male-male sexual activity while on the island very secret thus far, and if this Norwegian hunk had been in my small circles of special friends, I most certainly would have remembered that.

"Yes, at the Ledra Palace. You were checking out my basket. Did you like what you saw?"

"I . . . I." My mind was racing trying to figure out what he meant. And then it clicked, and I blushed and wasn't fast enough to disabuse him of the reason why I had been smiling up at the hotel façade. Svend took my blush as a "yes," and he swung a beefy arm around my shoulders in a possessive gesture, sure of himself, an assumption he every reason to make. I was lost to him.

He was whispering in my ear. "I've been hoping to see you in this bar. I would very much like to be with you, but my friends over there have bet among themselves that you couldn't take me."

"Be with me?" I asked dumbly.

"Yes, you are a beautiful man. I would like to fuck you. But I may be too big for you. At least that's what my friends are betting."

Fifteen minutes later I found myself naked on top of a pool table in a back room of the bar, with an applauding and appreciative audience, while Svend and I proved that I could, indeed, take more than two inches in diameter and not exactly stubby either. Svend called out the changing positions with glee as he took me every which way for a good thirty minutes. He was particularly pleased because he had bet on my capabilities.

For the next year until the Norwegian Stallions got rotated out and replaced with another UN unit, I gladly played toy to the playfulness and inventiveness of my own Norwegian stallion. Svend liked to take me by surprise and in unusual venues and circumstances—and he was always particularly pleased if there were unsuspecting people nearby, just a step away from where we were fucking. He learned quickly that I was quite vocal during sex, and he got a perverse pleasure out of me trying to hold back my cries of passion while that extraordinarily thick cock was churning inside me.

It seemed that he knew just when I'd be available to him but somewhere that I wouldn't suspect I was about to be ravished. Thus, once when I turned off the road down to the northern coastal town of Kyrenia and drove up the mountain instead for a few quiet moments in the ruins of the crusader castle of the d'Ibelins, St. Hilarion, Svend found me there and dragged me up to the high tower, bent me out of a window opening, and pumped me from behind, while I watched a family picnicking in the dell below and tried to keep from moaning too loudly. As he mined my ass deeply, I hoped they neither could hear my suppressed whimperings of that giant tool working around inside me or that they would look up and see me in the window. Svend had left my shirt on, but they could have told at a glance at my facial expressions of wanton ecstasy, if they could see detail from that far, that I was being royally fucked.

At another time, when my wife and I had joined an embassy personnel outing for the day to a combination pool, bar, and outdoor dining area above a beach on the island's rugged northern coast, Svend and some of his fellow soldiers were also there. And after exuding charm in introducing himself to my wife and my ambassador for the first time and having passed himself off as a casual tennis partner of mine at the Elian Club, Svend coaxed me to follow him at a distance into the sea. Standing there together, he close in behind me, in water up to our chests but within sight of those frolicking around the pool bar, including my wife and the ambassador, he pulled my butt back onto his engorged tool and held my hips to him with his strong hands as he fucked up into me in the water with local swimmers moving all about us.

I could say that these intrusions and this controlling of not only my body but my responses of being thickly fucked irritated me to the point where I put him in his place. But that, of course, wasn't the case at all. I was mesmerized by him—as much by his grinning bear attitude as by his superb cocksmanship. His exuberance was intoxicating. I had drifted to wanting men at least a decade older than I was, but still well muscled, to be working my body. Svend was younger, and almost like a puppy dog in his enthusiastic fucking, and I found his playfulness—and seeking of a sense of danger—especially fresh and arousing. I loved the surprise and danger of it as much as he did, and he was so well equipped that I obsessed with accepting that the proper place for him was burying his thick rod inside me in inventive positions and unseemly circumstances.

Once when some embassy colleagues and I were taking a visiting congressional delegation out to a dinner in a rooftop restaurant above the seaside and overlooking the ruins of the Byzantine Bellapais Abbey, somehow Svend was there and convinced a waiter friend to tell me I had an important telephone call. When I went to the booth, there was Svend, and he wanted me to sit on his cock right there in the telephone booth. But I persuaded him that this was just too dangerous and went back to the table to tell my colleagues I'd been called away on an emergency. And then Svend pulled me back into a closed section of the restaurant, separated from the active section only by bamboo screening, and he pulled me into his lap and fucked me not more than twenty feet from where the congressional delegation was finishing its meal, the thumb of one hand in my mouth being sucked, the fingers of the other hand pinching and rolling my nipples and his cock churning up inside me. When I felt I couldn't hold back a scream of passion and complete possession and of being stuffed any longer, he replaced his thumb with his lips and swallowed my cries with his searching kisses.

My strangest ravishing by the Norwegian stallion was when I went for a haircut from my regular barber in a hotel arcade. Svend came in to do the barber, who was just one of Svend's many man toys, and saw me there in the chair. He sent the barber to guard the door and then took me long and hard, first with my legs bent over the arms of the barber's chair and him standing on the metal foot ledge and then with me bent over the back of the chair and my knees on the arms and him crouched on the chair behind me. Then, with me sitting on his cock, my back to his front, he took shaving cream and creamed my chest and shaved off my thin trail of hair there with a straight razor, with me trying my best to hold steady on his digging tool. He said, with a laugh, that he was doing this for me to "remember him by." I thought this was a strange thing for him to say, because of course I was going to remember him by the thickness of his cock and his playfulness in finding new places and ways to master me.

That had been the day he found out his unit was being rotated out. But he didn't tell me about this on the day of the barbering. He called me a week later and told me he was coming by to see me. And, for the first time I decided to give *him* a surprise.

My house was a typical Mediterranean stucco pile with a red tile roof sitting high on a mesa overlooking the capital city and the Green Line, running like an open sore through the country, separating Greek from Turk. But the house also had some modern features. One was that the spiral stone staircase to the second level was encased in a semicircular opaque glass-brick wall. From the outside you could make out that someone was on the staircase, but the glass was too opaque to pick up much detail, although you could do so more at night with the lights on in the staircase than you could during the day. The staircase was located right next to the entry door.

It was near dusk when Svend pulled up on his motorbike. I had stripped already, and as he approached the door, I moved onto the stairs next to the entry and pushed my cock and belly and chest and lips right up against the opaque glass, so that he could clearly see just those parts of me, offering myself to him through the glass.

I never knew a man that large to be able to move that fast through an entry door and to strip down en route to the staircase, where, in full desire and rut, he laid me out on the stone risers and devoured my body with his. Thinking that the staircase routine was only foreplay and that we'd move to an upstairs bedroom for sex, I initially tried to fend him off and point out that our silhouettes could be seen from the valley below. But he just laughed and said, "All the better. Let them watch." And he was right, the sex was all the better for the danger of being seen. Ever since I've thought back on that encounter occasionally and wished that I had seen the silhouettes of him crouched over me on the staircase, my legs wrapped around his waist, and him fucking me.

He was almost sobbing when he was finished, and, for the first time since my initial ravishing by him on the pool table, I was able to give full vocalizing of my passion for what he was doing to my body. And that's when he let it all pour out that this was our last meeting, that his unit was being released of its UN obligations in two days' time, and that he was headed back to Oslo.

I missed his surprises for a good long time, but I never again let a man dominate and control me as he had for as long as he had. That life was just too dangerous for me to indulge in. Oh, and I missed that inhumanly thick cock for a long time too.

Chapter Nineteen: Turkish Delight Times Six

While living on the island of Cyprus, I developed quite a taste for young Turkish men. If you could get a good-looking, well-constructed Turkish guy before he got too far into his forties, you could almost guarantee you'd have something forceful, vigorous, straightforward, and good natured to play with. You also, quite often, would have a guy with a pretty heavy pelt on him. Now, I didn't particularly favor a hairy guy, but on a Turk, it could be quite arousing, and sometimes I just felt like rubbing my nipples against a fine chest of hair.

Cyprus is a divided island, with the southern two thirds being in Greek hands and the northern, more isolated, third in Turkish hands, with a UN-guarded "Green" zone separating the two belligerent sides. I was able to go back and forth between the sides with my job and had been on the island long enough to see that both Greek and Turkish young men had their good points. I quickly found, though, that the Turks—at least the Turkish Cypriots—had fewer inhibitions against male-male activity than the Greek Cypriots did as a rule, despite the historical reputation of the Greeks, although it was never difficult to make a hook up of either. The Turkish men were just more matter of fact and lusty in their fucking and weren't given to long drawn-out preliminaries if they saw something they were interested in.

Thus it was that the first opportunity for a weekend alone on the Turkish side, I was off and running. My wife and kids were in Athens for five days, over a weekend, and so I decided it was time for me to check up on the office on the Turkish side one Friday and just to stay over at the Turkish Cypriot seaside for the weekend.

After a brief Friday-afternoon appearance at the office in the Turkish sector of Nicosia, the capital—which the Turks called Lefkosa, I was racing my BMW convertible across the width of the island to the remote Salamis Bay Hotel. This hotel sat on a rocky beach at the edge of the ancient ruins of the Greek city of Salamis, which had been founded by the Greek troops returning from the sack of Troy and had been destroyed by an earthquake and largely reclaimed by the Mediterranean Sea in the third century B.C. I had picked this destination because it was in a remote corner of the island, where it was unlikely I'd be recognized, it boasted an infamous nude tourist beach, and I had been given the address of a small gay bar near the hotel. I wanted to make the most of my free weekend on the Turkish side.

When I got to the eastern end of the island, I got off the not-so-good direct road to Salamis onto the really-not-so-good coastal road so that I could locate the bar I wanted to go to that evening. I found it by following the really bad music of a live band gearing up in the twilight hour before the sun sank below the Troodos Mountains at the other end of the island. It was a beach bar composed of beverage carts surrounded by bar stools, under grass umbrellas around an ill-kept swimming pool on a terrace that went out over the Mediterranean. The enclosure was barely sectioned off from the view of the road by a scraggly bamboo-slatted fence. I could see that guys were already arriving for the evening; it looked like a young crowd and mostly the queen type, although I saw some well-cut studs among them. I could see that the typical attire was on the minimalist side. I stopped the BMW at the side of the road near the entrance to the bar to get a better look, and one of the more studly of the youngsters, a lithe, dark-but smooth-skinned guy appearing to be nineteen or twenty whistled and came over to the car. From the way he was looking the car over, I could tell he was whistling at the machine, not at me. But he at least was polite enough to ask me, with a toothy grin and a leer, if I was coming into the bar, and I told him I might drop back later.

The Salamis Bay Hotel, a seven-story balconied building that would have looked out of place on this desolate coast if it hadn't itself lacked a renovation in two decades, was only about a ten-minute drive from the bar. I stopped in the lobby bar for a beer to knock away the dust of the road between Lefkosa and the coast and then went up to my seventh-floor suite. I suppose they called this a suite because I had my own bathroom, but it was fine for my purposes. I'm sure the diplomatic plates on my BMW had something to do the relative royal treatment I was getting here, although, of course, I registered under a false name. There was a carpet on the floor that didn't look too mildewed, I may have gotten the only queen-sized bed in the hotel, and there was an expansive balcony overlooking the Salamis ruins and that would afford a spectacular view of sunrise over the Mediterranean—if I was awake at sunrise.

With a view to the attire I'd seen entering the gay beach bar, I opted for low-rise cut-offs and sandals, a money clip, a couple of condoms, and my car keys—and nothing else, including briefs. I wasn't here to do much shopping; I was here to get laid.

The music in the bar was still bad when I got there, but it was a whole lot louder than it had been before, and there was a whole lot larger crowd too, swaying to the music, hips close together, or swimming—and, I could tell, fucking—in shadows in the central swimming pool. Cheap strobe lighting was flitting around everywhere, making the patrons frenetically multicolored and helping to mask where they had their hands. I could tell I was making quite a stir in the place as an alluring foreign element, and a path parted between me and one of the bars under the grass umbrellas as I walked in. I asked for an Efes beer, and my American accent made the whole place my bosom buddy. Within seconds, I had the best of what I could see sniffing around me, looking for an opening. I gave the eye nod to a heavily muscled construction worker type in badly worn jeans and a black muscle T-shirt with a Harley-Davidson logo that must have set him back a week's pay. He was handsome in an ugly "don't mess with me" sort of way, swarthy of skin, with a two-day's growth of beard, and coarse, curly black hair trying to escape from every opening in his T. Just the change of pace I was in the mood for.

Half way through my Efes, he was sitting on a bar stool, with his legs around my hips and pulling my butt into his hard basket. He was moving my pelvis around on his crotch to the beat of the music, and I could feel that he wanted me in the worst way. Another quite acceptable candidate was trying to get my attention. He was standing close into the front of me. He had a palm of one hand over one of my nipples and took my beer bottle from me with his other hand and poked his tongue into it suggestively and gave me a lot of "cum hither" eye work. He handed the bottle back to me and was moving his face into mine, probably for a sloppy kiss, when there was a deep-grunted challenge from the guy who was lapping me and a beefy arm came out and pushed the challenger away. The battle for my attention seemed to be over then.

I still hadn't finished my beer when my host snaked his hand around, pushed it under my waistband, and held me close to his pushing cock with a skin-on-skin grip on my cock and balls. Then he was unbuttoning and unzipping my cut-offs with his other hand, and I think he would have fucked me right there and then on the bar stool, if I hadn't taken charge and removed his hands and told him that if he wanted to fuck me he'd have to come back to my hotel room. He didn't like that idea, but I started making eye contact with the next best candidates nearby, and he said that, OK, he'd leave the bar with me.

When we got out into the parking lot, the young stud from earlier in the day was sitting on the trunk of my BMW. He looked disappointed when he saw me coming out with another guy—a guy who easily could have snapped him in two. As we were getting in the car, though, I told the young guy I was staying at the Salamis Bay Hotel, and if he wanted to take a ride in my convertible and was in front of the hotel Sunday morning, I might be able to give him one. He seemed quite satisfied with that and waved vigorously as we pulled out of the parking lot.

My "date" asked me to stop the car and let him out before we got to the hotel entrance. He said he was known there and not particularly welcome and would have to come up the back stairs. I gave him my room number and left him there at the side of the road.

He arrived at my room door almost before I did. He had his hands all over me and was starting to wrestle me to the carpet as soon as I let him in the door and shut it, but I told him he would have to both shower thoroughly and use a condom if he wanted to fuck me. This didn't set well with him, but I managed to get him into the bathroom and declined his demand that I come in with him, although I said I'd be taking a shower before we fucked too. I asked him if he'd brought a condom, and he gave me a negative, sinister look. I was to find that the Turkish men wouldn't voluntarily use protection. This guy told me condoms were unmanly while he glowered at me. I told him he'd either have to use one or leave, and I was a little scared he'd just take me there on his own terms. He certainly could have done that, but perhaps whatever trouble he was in with the hotel combined with having to deal with an American, with unknown but highly probable clout, was keeping him in line, if only barely.

After he'd showered, he padded out into the room naked, and I saw that I had picked pretty well. His cock wasn't overly sized, but it was quite serviceable, and his body was beautifully shaped. As a bonus the heavy pelting on him was intriguing and gave my cock a little lurch. It was going to be like being fucked by a wild bear. I was game to try that.

I took no chances and locked the bathroom door while I showered and cleaned myself out well. When I came back into the room, expecting to see him stretched out on the bed, the room was empty. Then I saw him, sitting, still naked, out on the balcony, sulking at what he had to do to get some tail. I grabbed and opened a condom packet and picked up a tube of lube and came out on the balcony. He lost his sulk when I dropped my towel and he saw what a good deal he was getting. We engaged in our first kiss, me standing over him, while I rolled the condom on his erect dick and lathered lube over his tool. Then, knowing he wasn't going to put up with further delay, I straddled his thighs, facing him, positioned his cock at my back door, and descended on his manhood. He let out a hissing sound as I sheathed his cock, and I helped his mouth find one of my nipples.

I slid up and down on his pole for a few minutes, with him making grunting sounds that increased in intensity. I didn't figure that he was going to allow me control for very long like this, and I was right. With a primeval, guttural sound from deep inside him, He stood, briefly losing purchase in my ass with his cock, and carried me into the bedroom, slammed me down on my belly on the bed, got one of my arms in a hammer lock behind my back, forced my legs apart with his knees, positioned his cock at the entrance of my hole with his other hand, and then dove his cock into me. I screamed and nearly arched my body off of the surface of the bed as he tunneled his way up me, pounding me and pounding me, showing me who was the boss. Half way to lift off, he released my arm from his grip, circled his hands under my pelvis, sheathed my cock in one hand and cupped my balls in the other, and fairly lifted my feet off the floor as he pumped me back and forth on his cock.

When we'd both shot off, he fell on top of me and lay there, both of us heaving, until our breathing became regularized. Then he pulled off me, put his clothes back on, gave me a big grin of thanks, and was gone. Honest and straightforward. We'd both gotten what we wanted with a minimum of fuss. I hadn't expected him to stay the night or anything, and the intensity of the fuck had made me just as glad that he didn't stay around to do it again. But my guess was that he really didn't want to be caught in the hotel or inside one of its patrons and was headed back to the beach bar for his next fuck.

I was awake to catch the sunrise on my balcony after all, and a spectacular view it was.

I breakfasted in the hotel dining room, and the food wasn't half bad. While I was eating, I noticed a well-turned waiter giving me the once over more than once, and I almost choked on my coffee when I realized he had been one of "next best alternatives" in my bar hop of the previous evening. I filed his presence away as a possible chapter in my Turk weekend.

Then it was out to the nude tourist beach. Both Greek and Turkish societies are puritanical, but both are also highly entrepreneurial. There were nude beaches in both sectors of the island, but, by law, they were restricted to the foreign tourists, and the locals supposedly were limited to watching from the far-off fringes with binoculars. This being the Mediterranean, however, a local could get onto the beach just by paying off the police who were there to keep them away and also to see that there was no actual, graphic sex acts being performed on the beach. Heavy petting didn't seem to violate this law, but maybe the police guards on duty just considered permitting that to be a fringe benefit for themselves. In another anomaly of the Greek and Turkish systems on this, woman nude tourists were just to be ogled, on pain of serious punishment, but nude men tourists were accepted as advertising their availability.

Thus it was that when I arrived at the beach and set out my towel and then stripped off my skimpy Speedo—the same size Speedo I had used for months to build up a very nice tan—what was left untanned became pretty much a billboard, and a nice enough advertisement that I was surrounded by men of several different nationalities in no time flat. This was to be a Turk weekend, though, so I waved off the Scandinavians and Israelis and concentrated on the Turkish possibilities. Several of these men looked like they would do, and I tried a few out with some hands work—theirs on me and mine on them—an activity they didn't seem to mind sharing—and the local police didn't mind watching. Four young men seemed to arouse me sufficiently, and when I'd brought up the condom requirement and asked if they had come prepared, I was down to two.

Rather than make choices between these two, when I couldn't really tell much of a difference between them except that one had a slightly bigger cock than the other, I just named them Turk A (nice cock) and Turk B (nicer cock) and asked what we

141

were to do about the no sex on the beach rule and the roving police. They both laughed, gathered up a large beach towel and me, and hustled me down to the water. We entered the water and moved around a rock formation, where there was a little cover surrounded by smooth rocks, a place that could not be seen from the beach.

Turk A stretched his towel out on one of these rocks, and the three of us loosened each other up with several minutes of mutual admiration of body parts and stroking and sucking of same, accompanied by much kissing and good-natured laughing. At length, Turk A pushed me on my back on the towel and I opened my legs wide for him and let him prepare my asshole for his onslaught. I made sure he was sheathed by rolling a condom on him myself, and then Turk B stretched out beside me and played with my nipples and cock and balls while Turk A fucked me as vigorously as my "date" from the previous evening had. When both he and I had come, I rolled a condom onto Turk B and, at his direction, waded out into the water with him. When we were standing in water nearly up to our nipples, I climbed his torso in the buoyant water, wrapping my legs around his waist and helping him to insert his nicer cock in my ass, and he fucked up into me there in the turquoise-blue, calm Mediterranean.

When we returned to the beach, I was exhausted enough from the attention from those two Turks that I pulled my Speedo back on and just lay baking in the sun, fully satisfied with how my weekend was going.

Before the afternoon was over I found out why the local police were so forgiving of sexual activity on the beach. I was still being propositioned by a bevy of young guys when a policeman came up to us. The guys scattered and I thought maybe I'd be given some grief, but the cop, another young, highly presentable Turk, simply smiled shyly at me and told me what he'd like to do and showed me that he'd even brought his own condom. I didn't want to get in the bad graces of anyone in authority, and he really was quite nice looking and polite, so I let him lead me over to a shed where the beach protectors went to get out of the sun. He fucked me from behind up against the wall, making very pleased sounds through the whole coupling.

When I entered the hotel from my jaunt on the beach, the "another nice candidate" hotel employee was waiting for me in the lobby. He hailed me as I was crossing to the elevator and asked me, in a very pointed tone, if there was anything he could do to make my stay more comfortable or memorable. I told him I was on my way to my room to take a shower and told him that if he was a masseur or knew of one, sure, I could use a little work on my muscles. While I was showering, he used his pass key and joined me under the spray. Taking my offhand remark to heart, he did a little work on the muscle between my legs there, and then brought me out to the bed, laid me on my belly, and started massaging my shoulder muscles. This only lasted for about twenty seconds before we were rolling around on the bed together and arrived in a 69 position, where we slowly sucked each other off. Then we rolled around some more, and when he'd reloaded, he straddled my hips from behind, his hands holding my arms down on the surface of the bed, and fucked me with what I was learning was typical Turk vigor and enthusiasm and with what I'm sure was the longest cock I took that weekend. He at least stayed around long enough after the main event for me to run my hands through a Turkish pelt, from chest to pubes. At my invitation, he came back and had me for dessert after I'd eaten dinner in the hotel dining room and slept half the night with me in my hotel bed, proving several times in the night that a Turk can be tender and forceful at the same time.

Sunday morning I had set aside to explore the ruins at Salamis, but when I walked out of the entrance of the hotel, there sat the grinning young Turk I had encountered two days previously at the gay beach bar entrance. He was sitting on the trunk of my car, in expectation of that ride I had promised him. So, I decided to explore him before exploring the ruins and took him for a long ride in the BMW with the top down, stopping and lingering in a little copse of trees well off the road at the edge of the Mediterranean, where I then took him into the backseat of my car and rode him to exhaustion. I had a bigger and longer dick than any I'd seen on a Turk that weekend, and he squealed with delight as I split him asunder and found out that Turks were as good at receiving as giving.

Chapter Twenty: Someday My Prince Will . . .

Last night I dreamed I went to paradise again. I believe we can credit the encounter to Daphne du Maurier. My tour in Cyprus was at an end, but I had hung on for a month, sending my wife back to Washington, D.C., to get the house open up again and everything there back in working order and to guide one of our children into a new university year. I had stayed past my assignment rotation date to attend an artists' gathering in the Troodos mountain village of Platres. A internationally well-known naive artist lived there during her summers and held an annual week-long artists' retreat there. I had been invited to the retreat because I had just published a novel based loosely on her intriguing life and she had done the cover for the book. We got along famously, and so here I was, gathered with her artist friends and trying to keep up with the talk of light and shadow and balance and depth perception—not unknown concepts for the creative writer either, I happily realized.

The artists were dotted around in various residences in the rustic mountain village and met in the afternoons at the artist's rambling and cool house for discussions and then at 10:30 p.m. each evening at the central open-air restaurant to celebrate their talent in local wine and a meze, which was a never-ending march of finger foods across the table top. After this, they dragged back to their host homes and slept until the next afternoon's gathering at the artist's home.

I opted for other lodging, however. I was leaving a country I loved and wanted to make the most of every moment I could. There was a fine old, internationally known English-style hotel, the Forest Park, at the edge of Platres, high on a hill. I opted for that partially, but not solely, for its somewhat dishabille opulence but also because of the room I requested and was able to book—the suite where Daphne du Maurier wrote the draft of her classic novel, *Rebecca*.

I had just begun to learn what my direction would be after a career of spying, thanks to the success of my novel, and I wanted to seek inspiration in the room where *Rebecca* had been drafted—perhaps even conceived. This had already worked well when I had managed to rent the home of Lawrence Durrell on the island's northern coast, where he wrote much of his *Alexandria Quartet*. So, I was seeking a muse. I would never have imagined to have also found a prince.

He knocked on my door at the Forest Park late on the morning after I had arrived and politely asked if he might just have a look at the room. He introduced himself as Gregor and said he was a student, majoring in creative writing, and wanted just to see where Du Maurier had worked the magic of her pen. Thus, he was established immediately as a fellow seeker.

Over lunch on the large, tiered stone terrace at the back of the hotel, I learned that there were several other parts to his name, with the one that really rang a bell being Hapsburg. He acknowledged he was of those Hapsburgs and was, in fact, a prince on paper, although he'd never been permitted to see what would have been his domain in Hungary if a couple of world wars had not interceded.

He was a very presentable young man of solid build, handsome features other than a very prominent jaw that I was to learn was the genetic curse of his family, pale blue eyes, and an exuberance of dark hair leaping from his head in an unruly, but not unattractive fashion. He was a wonderful conversationalist, and I was already going over the artist retreat scheduling in my mind to determine when I could possibly see him again, when he obviated my efforts. While my mind had been spinning, I asked him what he was doing here in Cyprus other than pilgrimaging to famous writers' dens.

"The contrast of sporting interests," he answered with a winsome smile.

"Excuse me?" I asked. "What sports would those be?"

"I want to snow ski and swim in the ocean on the same day."

"And you can do that here?" I asked, not really believing his answer, thinking he was just being flippantly sparkly in his conversation.

"Yes. There is a minimal ski slope up on Mt. Olympus, no more than a three-quarters hour drive away from here. There's usually enough natural snow this late in the season, but if there isn't, they just make it. It's cold enough up there. And then in just about an hour I can be down at Pissouri Beach from here and swim in the Mediterranean."

"I don't believe it," I said, somewhat lamely. There was no reason for me to doubt him really, but I'd been in the country for years and hadn't heard about the skiing. But then the topic would rarely have come up when discussing a mostly dusty and warm Mediterranean island. The Scandinavians came here to swim on New Year's Day.

"I can prove it, if you're game," Gregor said. "Come with me tomorrow, and we'll ski in the morning and then go down and swim in the sea in the afternoon."

It was an invitation I couldn't refuse. I'd been on Cyprus for a couple of years and hadn't realized this could be done. This would be my last chance of doing it so that I'd have the story to tell when I returned to the States. The artists wouldn't miss me for their afternoon session, and I'm sure they'd be as delighted with Gregor as I was if I brought him to the evening celebration.

Gregor was right. We skied in the morning on Mt. Olympus, although the slopes were such that it was more for the novelty of the activity than for the exercise or the downhill racing

147

thrill. And we were down on the somewhat rough-rocked Pissouri Beach shore by noon. We swam for a bit and then lay out on beach towels on the shale side by side and talked of writing and European history and of art while we dried off. We studiously avoided talking of anything intimate, but our Speedos had no chance of hiding from each other our increasing interest one for the other. Gregor was well muscled, if a little simian, with short, strong legs on a well-proportioned and slightly hirsute torso, and long arms with fine-fingered, sensuous artist's hands.

Acknowledging almost at the same time that we were hungry, we moved up to a seaside open-air café and ordered up swarmas, a luscious pita bread sandwich filled with shaved roasted beef slathered with tahini sauce. The young Greek waiter serving us seemed well taken with Gregor and he with the waiter, and they flirted unabashedly while we ate. Gregor finished his swarma before I did and excused himself for a few moments. When I finished, I went to what passed for a men's room, which was more a hole in the ground in a section separated off the back of the café and enclosed by lattice work covered with grape vines.

I could see through the latticework as I pissed in the hole, and I spied Gregor kneeling in front of the Greek waiter, who was leaning against the back wall of the café. Gregor was giving the waiter deep and rhythmic head, and the waiter was loving it. There was something about the prominent Hapsburg jaw working on a nice, hard cock that was mesmerizing. I knew that at some point in this brief encounter with the prince that I wanted some of that for myself.

The waiter returned to the table several minutes before Gregor reappeared, and the young man was smiling and humming a happy tune to himself, which well he might. I wasn't very surprised Gregor didn't appear first. He gave me plenty of time to receive and pay the bill for lunch; I had gotten the drift of who would pay earlier in the day when I managed to have my wallet out first at every turn of the skiing experience. And, of course, we drove in my BMW convertible. Gregor claimed this was because he'd fallen in love with the car, but I suspected that Gregor had no real transportation of his own. There was no loss on the lunch bill, though. The well-satisfied waiter hadn't charged for Gregor's meal.

That evening in the town square open-air restaurant under the bright stars peeking through the swaying pine trees and the cool breezes coming down from Mt. Olympus in this otherwise frying pan island at the start of summer, the atmosphere was festive and electric. Artists know how to have a good time and how to remain convivial as they sank deeper and deeper into drink. Gregor, who, of course, I brought and who, of course, was instantaneously and enthusiastically adopted by the artists, was particularly convivial with a usually very serious young abstract painter who I'd always thought took himself a bit too seriously.

About midway through the evening, which didn't end until nearly 4 a.m., I noted the prolonged absence of both Gregor and the abstract painter, and it didn't take me long to find them in a small grove just steps away from the illumination of the strings of white Christmas tree lights that defined the restaurant perimeter from the stone-lined streets sloping up and down around it at precarious angles.

Gregor was vigorously pumping the abstract painter's cock with his strong jaw, and the painter was bucking wildly against him, at the height of ecstasy, no longer a bit aloof, off on some level of his own in the fireworks of passion. Gregor finished the other young man in a flooding of cum and a stifled cry of release, and I left them there, kissing deeply in the shadows.

This, of course, did not decrease my tension and anticipation as the party broke up and Gregor followed me back up the hill on foot to the towering Forest Park. I didn't question why he was still in step with me and would have gone breathless if he'd made any movement to leave my side. But he didn't; he walked me to the door to my room and thanked me very politely for accompanying him on his daily adventures and especially for bringing him into the circle of my artist friends.

We lingered there, not saying anything, and he turned to leave, not being able to continue the conversation. I was completely choked up. I wanted to ask him to come in, but I'd never pursued a man in my life and had such a strong sense of a code on this not to start now. I felt that this was when I'd start going downhill into over the hill in these male-male relationships. I didn't want to become a pitiful beyond-the-age-of-desirability man begging for it.

I watched in despair as Gregor turned and moved down the corridor. But then, just as I had opened my door and was about to move into the room—probably to be upset with myself for the remainder of the week—he turned and gave me a shy smile.

"Actually, I have no idea where I'm going," he said. "I made no arrangements for the night. I'm afraid it's the Hapsburg in me, the family trait of living off the people. Could you possibly . . .?"

I swung the door open wide, and we barely had it closed behind us when we were at each other, devouring each other, our hands and lips racing to discover all they could of the curves and crevices of each other—the points at which a sensuous moan, sigh, or groan could be teased out of the other.

He had my trousers off my legs, and I was experiencing firsthand the honor of the Hapsburg jaw wrapped around a cock that had been ready for him, aching for him, since early that afternoon on the beach. That Hapsburg jaw for which dynasty was mocked for generations was a tumultuous love-making vessel for me. I fell back against the wall beside the door as his warm, sensuous, experienced mouth played symphonies of pleasure on my throbbing member and balls.

I came quickly, having dreamed of this all day, and then I pulled him up and turned him belly to the wall, pushed his trousers down, and pulled his dick through the wide stance he had taken with his well-muscled thighs. He groaned, cheek planted against wallpaper, and beat his fists lightly against the wall while I alternated between giving him head on his pulled-thorough cock and wetting and loosening up his puckered hole with my lips and fingers.

When his hole was gaping and he was begging for it, I frog-marched him over to the bed, pushed him down on his back, spread his legs wide, thrust inside him, and fucked him until we were both spent in great shootings of cream.

We then stripped completely, showered and toweled off together, and shared the bed, him now taking me in a slow, languid side split of divine pumping that lasted until the dawn.

We slept soundly—or at least I did. I slept so soundly and satisfied and filled that when I awoke, I discovered that Gregor was gone and there was no trace of him except for a note written on Forest Park stationery and laid on what a plaque claimed was the very writing desk where Du Maurier had penned her famous novel of romance, lust, and eventual exile. In a few brief, messy, yet masterful strokes, Gregor had written of how enjoyable and memorable the time with me had been. His signature, surely the full name he was given, took up more room than the well-received sentiments he had left me with. And I remember at the time chuckling and wondering if his autograph would ever be worth what I had spent on him.

But, no matter. My prince had come—and come and come—in the most delightful and memorable way.

Chapter Twenty-One: Ride 'Em Cowboy

Since the 1930s my extended family has had a remote ranch in a hidden Colorado Rockies valley abutting Medicine Bow National Park south from Laramie, Wyoming. The mountain fasts there—almost alpine in environment—are majestic, but they can be raw and cruel as well.

Our family raised cattle there and took timber off the mountainsides in a planned "thinning" harvest pattern that supported a construction business down in Denver without denuding the forested hillsides. We weren't year-round ranchers, though, eschewing the forbidding winters by centering our lives elsewhere and only using the oft-expanded rambling stone and log ranch house for periodic vacations. Anyone in the family corporation could show up at the ranch after merely checking to see how many others would be in temporary residence; the rest of the year the ranch was taken care of by a long-term foreman and a succession of young—and not so young—wranglers holding fast to the dream of the wild and independent American West cowboy.

These cowboys were a sturdy, if somewhat rough and self-absorbed lot, many of whom had accommodated to the life of isolation in a wild and remote wilderness by taking whatever opportunities came their way.

Thus it was that, having called ahead to report that I was on home leave from a European tour and planned to take a Colorado rest and recuperation by riding the range and fishing the cold mountain trout streams, I found Big Bill, a handsome, if wind-chiseled-featured, rangy cowboy of almost indeterminate age hunched over the railing of the stable fence, waiting for me to arrive. He was leaning his lithe and sinewy hard-worked body over the fence with one booted foot on the lower rail and spinning a stalk of oats in his mouth when I caught sight of him. A big grin spread across his creased, weather-beaten face when I drove up in a Jeep Cherokee in a cloud of dust and came to a sliding stop beside the covered log veranda extending across the wide face of the ranch house. A hunky hulk of a young blond I'd never seen before was keeping him company at the rail.

"Heard yer were comin' into the valley, Mr. H.," Big Bill called out to me. I walked over toward him, and he stood up straighter as I did and set his creased and oily cowboy hat back on his head so that I could see the glint of welcome in his eyes.

"Yep," I replied. "Got a little tired of being targeted by all those bombs on my forays into the Middle East," I said, with a grin. "Thought I'd come back here for a spell and check out whether there are any missiles here as threatening as those I encountered in Lebanon."

"I reckon we can find a few here if that's what you want," Big Bill responded, with a hearty laugh. "Come for another ride, did you? Wantin' to go up into the hills again like we did last summer?"

"Yeah, that's exactly what I want," I answered. "I need some tension release. I figure a good ride and then several hours in the trout stream will help a lot."

"Doesn't look like you brought the family," Big Bill said.

"Nope. The wife couldn't get away. She's still back in D.C."

"So, it's just you, is it?" Bill asked.

"Yep. Any of the rest of the family in residence?"

"Not for another week or so. Most of the Colorado family will come in when the leaves have hit their peak of fall color. That shouldn't be for another week or two."

"So, it's just us, is it?"

"Yep, most of the workers have the week off to set up for the long fall run of family in the house. I'm yer cook and general handyman, I'm afraid."

"Suits me just fine," I said.

"So, do you still want to take that ride up in the hills rather than just staying down here?"

"Yes, and the sooner the better. Can you get the horses and all that we'll need together in the next hour or two? And supplies for sleeping out under the stars? I've been looking forward to this for months."

"I sure can," Big Bill responded. "But, uh, where are my manners. Jawing away like this, and not even introducing you to the new hand. Mr. H., this is Long Jack; Long Jack, Mr. H."

As we shook hands, my mind worked over what the "Long Jack" could mean. None of the cowboys went by their real names—in truth, most cowboys out here were escaping something or someone and had no intention of bandying their real names about. I'd found out where the "Big Bill" had come from last summer. I wondered what "Long Jack's" story was. Whatever it was, he was one muscled, blond hunk of a man. Probably Scandinavian in background; maybe over from Minnesota. And handsome. The sun and wind hadn't had time to etch his features yet. He beamed at me, obviously a very friendly fellow.

"And, do you mind of Long Jack comes along, Mr. H.? I think he'd like a ride too, if that's OK with you."

"Yeah, of course," I replied, all smiles. "I'd like that."

"I kinda thought you would," Big Bill said with a big grin.

Less than two hours later, we were in the saddle on three stallions and riding up the ridgeline of a spur rising up from the ranch house into the foothills of the Rockies to the west of the Medicine Bow parkland. This was gorgeous scenery, visited rarely by man. The trees were beginning to change color, but we were in a very warm spell—so warm that we all stripped off our shirts.

Although both hard bodied, Big Bill and Long Jack were a contrast in fine manhood. The older wrangler, black haired and on the edge of hirsute, was sinewy and on the thin side, with swarthy, leathery skin beaten by the cruel elements. His arms and chest were ropy, with veins standing out on top of hard muscle. Scaring on his body from various mishaps in this sometimes-cruel environment enhanced the "man" attraction of him. In contrast, the younger wrangler obviously hadn't been in the elements out here all that long. He was blond, fair, smooth skinned, and bulky without an apparent ounce of fat on him. He had a deep chest tapering down to a thin waist and biceps as thick as some men's waists. He probably could have broken me in two.

It was going to be an interesting ride.

Traveling west toward the Rockies as our horses climbed into the hills, we reached a high meadow where the air was so clear and clean and the distant snow-capped Mount Zirkel appeared so close that it gave the illusion we could reach out and touch it. Big Bill called a halt at a grassy spot beside a burbling creek, and I was still drinking in the majestic scenery when both Big Bill and Long Jack came down off their horses and approached mine from either side. Big Bill encircled my waist with his sinewy arms from one side of the horse and Long Jack placed his big hands on my belly and the small of my back; both men were smiling at me.

"You've kept yourself in mighty fine shape, Mr. H.," Big Bill said. "Is what you've got there in your pants as nice a piece as it was last summer?"

"Check it out for yourself," I answered.

"Don't mind if I do. You ready for a rough ride?"

"Of course. I've looked forward to it all the way from the East Coast."

As Big Bill was unzipping my jeans and fishing out my half-hard cock, Long Jack moved his hands up to my sternum and between my shoulder blades and pulled me flat across the back and croup of the horse. He kissed me deeply on the lips and played with my nipples, as Big Bill sucked my cock. The stallion held still, but it was trembling underneath me. Long Jack's mouth left mine and his lips traveled down to my nipples and then down across my navel, and he was joining Big Bill in mouthing my cock and balls. I laid there full length on the back of the horse, sighing and moaning and watching the snow-patterned ragged rocks of Mount Zirkel as the two wranglers shared my cock.

But then Big Bill got serious at sucking my tool and I looked around and saw that Long Jack had busied himself stripping the saddles off of the other two horses and laying them out in the middle of the grass clearing. Then he slowly stripped off his clothes, revealing a beautiful body-builder's physique. I could now see at least how he had gotten the "Long" part of his nickname. He came back and played my mouth and upper torso with his lips and hands again while Big Bill brought me to a groaning and moaning ejaculation with his insistent mouth.

When he was done, Big Bill's lips replaced those of Long Jack's on my lips. Then he whispered in my ear, "Are you ready for that ride now, Mr. H.?"

"Oh God yes," I replied. "I've been waiting for this for so long."

Big Bill pulled me off the horse and carried me over to one of the saddles resting in the center of the clearing. He stripped all of my clothes off except for my boots and the red bandana around my neck—and then he put my chaps on again, which left me bare at the pelvis fore and aft. He laid me across the dip in the saddle on my belly and tied my wrists to the stirrups of the saddle at each side with leather strips. After that, he stood where I could see him as he stripped down. His dong wasn't as long as Long Jack's, but it was much thicker, in keeping with his nickname. I moaned at the sight of it in remembrance of how he had plowed me the previous summer when I had visited these mountains.

He went over to the saddle bags on the other saddle and came back with a thick length of leather, a small riding crop, and several packets of condoms. Big Bill hunched down over me on the small of my back, his thick cock laying up between my shoulder blades. He brought the thick leather strap over my head and forced it into my mouth like a bit. Then he held the two ends of it like reins and pulled my head and back up to him in an arch and reached back with his other hand and started slapping me lightly on the buttocks as he rode my back, his cock rubbing up and down between my shoulder blades and mine rubbing up and down on the supple leather of the saddle seat. I could feel my back slicking up from the precum his cock was oozing as he stroked me. He rode me like a bucking horse like that for a while, eventually exchanging his hand slapping with flickings of the ride crop on my tender butt cheeks. He was making all of those rodeo shouts and gestures as he rode me. At length he reduced his gyrations to those of a trot, rubbing his cock up and down between my shoulder blades more deliberately; he stopped spanking and flicking my buttocks as I felt my butt cheeks being pulled apart and Long Jack tonguing and then fingering, with lubricant, my asshole.

Leaving Long Jack to prepare my ass for him, Big Bill stood beside me, and I watched him tear open a condom packet and sheath his monster cock with some difficulty. Then he was on my back again, rubbing the sheathed cock between my shoulder blades.

Long Jack's tongue and fingers disappeared and Big Bill slowly pulled his thick, now fully engorged cock back down along my spine until it dropped down into the crack between my butt cheeks and then was at my asshole. I arched my back against the reins and howled to the sky as he entered me with that huge cock and slowly plowed up my ass canal. When he was in to the root, he dropped the reins and I collapsed my head and chest onto the grass on the other side of the saddle and panted heavily at the filling and stretching of my canal.

"Oh God, oh God, you're splitting me," I cried.

"Do you want me to get off you?" Big Bill asked in a bit of confusion and concern. I was from the family; I could end his billet at the ranch with a snap of my fingers.

"Oh no, fuck me," I cried back at him. "I've been thinking of this for months. Fuck me hard."

And then I felt hands on my ankles; Long Jack was pulling my legs up and wishboning them, handling me like a wheelbarrow and opening me wider to Big Bill's tool and the older wrangler was riding my ass hard, just as I wanted him too. After a long, wild ride, he gave a little cry, quickly pulled out of me and pulled the sheath off and fired off across the small of my back. He rubbed the cum into my skin in strokings across my back with his still half-hard tool.

Long Jack was quickly untying my hands then, but not to free me. He pulled me up and turned me so that the small of my back was rising up the side of the saddle, my shoulder blades were flat on the grass, and my butt was suspended resting on the seat of the saddle and pointed toward the sky. Big Bill retied my wrists to the saddle stirrups while I watched Long Jack sheath his cock with a condom and then Big Bill and hunched over my chest, presenting his cock—moist from his man juice—for me to suck. I felt my legs being spread and Long Jack was snaking that long cock up into me and took his turn riding me long and vigorously while I bucked my pelvis up against his, meeting him stroke for stroke.

When Long Jack pulled out of me, ripped off his condom, and started to spout his semen all over my belly and the insides of my thighs, giving little cries of ecstasy all the while, I got the real point of his name—his ejaculation was unbelievably long and full. Big Bill freed me and we all ran down and splashed ourselves clean in cold mountain creek. As I was coming up out the water, though, Big Bill pushed me down onto my hands and knees in the grass and meadow flowers at the edge of the water and fucked me hard again doggie style. After he was done, I splashed back into the water and turned and watched Long Jack fuck Big Bill. They coupled like they did this regularly, which, no doubt, they did.

Big Bill cooked a meal over an open fire and we ate, stretched out against the saddles in the nude, as the warm late afternoon moved into a cooler twilight and the brilliant stars out in this mountain wilderness began to spread across the sky. The wranglers opened the sleeping bags then and spread them out, it being too warm to wrap ourselves in them considering the warmth we generated as Big Bill and Long Jack took turns riding me the whole night long out under a full moon glistening off the snowy Mount Zirkel peak.

The two wranglers managed to catch catnaps between fuckings, but they kept me awake all night. I didn't mind. I had been waiting for this for nearly a year—and that's when I thought I'd just have Big Bill to couple with. The blond stud was a real bonus.

Chapter Twenty-Two: Renewal of Passion

I had been down and just marking time ever since I'd left Beirut three years earlier. I hadn't really been able to write that whole time either; I was just floating on the royalties from my earlier novels, written in the passion of my youth—passion that I just couldn't find in me anymore. Perhaps it was having hit that deadly age of fifty; perhaps passion naturally dissipated from that point. But, again, perhaps it was the radical change in my lifestyle. I'd loved teaching at the American University of Beirut, but I'd been warned it was time to leave Lebanon—that it was just too dangerous there for Americans at that time—and I knew in my heart that this was a reasonable assessment—that placing myself in danger placed others around me in danger as well, people I cared deeply for. I'd loved—in every sense of the word—my young protégé, Riyad Munif, now a celebrated novelist throughout the Arab world in his own right. Three long years later now, and I hadn't had anyone since that last, memorable evening in Riyad's arms before I boarded my last flight out of Lebanon. The glorious memory of possessing him, my cock churning around inside him, and him moaning and sighing for me in that beautiful melodic voice of his—just a slowly receding memory. Now all I had was dry dust: mornings as an occasional guest lecturer at a creative writing class over at the university and afternoons and evenings sitting in front the blank, blinking window of my computer, spent of both words and passion.

It was on a cold, dreary morning in one of those creative writing classes that my Palestinian came into my life and thawed my frozen heart. He was bright eyed, hanging on my every word and nuance. And he was beautiful, all dark and steamy good looks. I was lost to men of the Levant; that, quite frankly was why I had landed in Beirut to begin with. In my youth, all you had to do is troop a young Arab beauty by me, and my cock would flip up to attention. But as beautiful as this young Palestinian student, Samir, was, my cock was just nestled there, limply down my right pant leg on this morning. I was feeling so old. So useless and empty.

But these feeling apparently didn't convey to Samir. As class was breaking up, he asked me if he could show me the manuscript he was working on, that he was blocked on how to proceed and really could use some help. I hesitated a few moments, knowing full well that I didn't have anything else to do that day—or the next day—or the day after that. He looked so eager and stroked my ego so hard with comments on the effect my novels had had on him, that I relented and took him back to my home with me that day.

While I sat in my wing chair, scanning through passages from his manuscript, Samir stretched out on my sofa, his eyes glued to mine, looking for any evidence of response, negative or positive to his writing.

Samir's style was vaguely familiar and was getting more and more familiar as I continued. His phrasing was elegant and sparse and the content was warming my blood, as I was pulled into the tale of a young student's love affair with his professor—his male professor. The character of the professor had such familiarity to it; it was almost as if I already knew this person. And Samir himself obviously was the narrator of the tale, the young student of the manuscript. I felt a stirring inside me that I hadn't felt for three years.

I looked up sharply at Samir. He was favoring me with a sensuous-lipped smile. I was a little shocked and confused. This was strongly homosexual material. Wonderfully written, but leaving little to the imagination. I'd never written anything but the most mainstream novels. Yet, this student was sitting here, watching me read his explicit prose without the least bit of embarrassment about how I might be reacting to the material.

"Excellent work, Samir," I said. "But these characters . . . some of this phrasing. They seem so familiar. Is this all your work? I can't place it, but . . ."

"Perhaps it is because of who I . . . studied . . . under."

I was confused. Why the hesitation? And why that languid grin?

"Riyad Munif," Samir explained as he gracefully unwound himself from a semisuppine position on the couch and sat up on the edge, very close to me now. "My undergraduate work was at the American University of Beirut—under Professor Riyad Munif. And I mean under professor Munif in more ways than one. Professor Munif told me about you when he learned I was coming to the States to study."

I sat there, dumbfounded, not able to say a thing. Old memories and emotions stirring. A sign of spring returning for the first time in three years.

Samir stood and took my hand in his and simply said, "Would you mind terribly if I took you into your bedroom and made love to you? It would mean so much to me and to my writing."

Shock. A complete lose for words or action. I dumbly rose as he squeezed my hand and followed him to my bedroom, where he slowly undressed me with his hands, covering me with his gliding and searching hands and mouth as he did so. When I was naked, he pushed me down into a sitting position on the edge of the bed and started working my cock with a soft and searching mouth. My fingers went to his head, wandering through his black, curly hair, and holding him to my crotch. I was having trouble breathing and gave him quite an audible show with my groans and moans as he brought me back to life after so many months and years of dormancy.

He pulled away only long enough to murmur, "Riyad was so right. He said you were huge and so thick. He was right. You don't know how I've dreamed about this cock." And then he was swallowing me again, deep-throating me, making me hold my breath to the point of blacking out. I shuddered and came down his throat in several spouting fountains of long-unsummoned semen.

The young, vigorous Samir popped right up, quickly stripped off his clothes, revealing a perfectly shaped body, lovingly built and maintained, and jumped up on the bed on his knees. Pulling me with him, he positioned us on the center of the bed and devoured me with kisses. His hands were everywhere, exploring my every curve and cavity, entering even my ass deep enough to reach my prostate and make my cock, so recently drained, harden up again and begin to burble precum. All the time he was telling me how wonderful my body was, sweet words for a fifty-year-old has been, even if untrue. Whatever the truth of the matter, his words and attention were having a marvelous effect. I felt the passion of arousal coursing through me again, after a long, long absence.

He lips and teeth were at my nipples now, ravaging them, making me crazy with lust.

"Riyad told me you loved nipple work," he was whispering. "And you have such large, brown aureoles. I can hardly get them in my mouth—but I will try." And try and succeed he did, and Riyad had been very right about my nipples as an erogenous zone, and I screamed out in ecstasy for him and writhed under my young attacker.

He had me on my back now and was below me, attacking my cock, balls, and asshole equally with his lips, tongue, teeth. My hips were bouncing up and down on the surface of the bed, in an ever-more-rapid rhythm. I was fucking his mouth again now with the rhythm of my hips and, at the same time, fucking myself on the three stiff fingers he had up my ass.

A flash of regret as my mind focused now on what was surely to happen next. Samir was going to fuck me. He was going to bury that lovely young dick up my ass and pump me hard. It had been so long since I'd had sex that I almost welcomed this. But I remember something I had frequently said when I, myself, was a young stud. "Young top turns into old bottom," I've always said. Samir had brought me back to life when I thought that sex was finally dead to me, but there was slight regret that I was to become a fulfillment of my old mocking declaration. It's the old man who gets fucked—if he's lucky.

Samir slid up my body, covering mine with his. "Fuck me now. Will you fuck me now?" he asked plaintively. "Riyad said you were a master cocksman. Can you side split me? Riyad said you were the best at that."

I was flooded with gratefulness and a new wave of passion that brought with it strength and confidence I hadn't experienced since I'd gotten on the plane in Beirut.

I turned on my side, and Samir nestled his body within mine, his butt cuddled into my crotch. As I lifted Samir's right leg up and away from his body with my hand, he reached down and guided my erect cock to and just inside his asshole, and then I started to assert control.

"Wait a minute," Samir suddenly said and bounced away from me and off the bed. "Do you mind if I tilt this dresser mirror so we both can see what you're doing? I want to watch your cock as it moves in and out of me."

He took the deep growling of overflowing passion at the back of my throat as assent and turned the mirror and was quickly back within my trembling arms. Old memories and capabilities and techniques and control and vigor returning to me, as my cock plowed up Samir's ass and I pumped him. With added fascination, I watched my thick cock stroking back and forth in his impossibly tight, sweet hole as the movement was reflected in the mirror. I turned my eyes on Samir's and saw him watching the movement with wide-eyed wonder. He groaned and whispered in a breathy small, voice, "God, that's hot. Watching you enter and pump me. Can you take it all out and stuff it back in again? Ahhh. Yes. And again, harder, deeper? Yessss! It's so Bi— Ahhhhhh, Yessss!" He was whimpering now, lost in the combined effect of sight and sensation.

Our lips met and devoured each others, both at the height of passion and lust.

At full power, I pulled him up onto his knees and held his hips in strong hands, rocking him back and forth as I continued to pump my cock inside him for long minutes. He screamed and cried and groaned and grunted, leaving no question of my virility and ability to grab him deep and pull all of the energy and passion out of him that he had to give. This old man mastering and exhausting the younger man writhing below me.

Leaving a satisfied Palestinian youth collapsed on my bed, moaning and whimpering his full satisfaction, I rose and moved to my computer and started to fill those empty screens with an elegant, bold story of passion and renewed power. Old no more in any dimension that counted.

Chapter Twenty-Three: At the Reservoir

I take three- to five-mile hikes about twice weekly. I have five nearby nature trails I rotate through (in addition to a few more urban walks). The park I went to recently—at the town's reservoir—has been on the Internet for years as a male pickup spot, although the police seemed to have stopped that a few years ago, I thought—and the pickup spots (the restrooms and an old barn) aren't near where I walk.

I was coming down a wooded trail slanting down to a bridge over a stream in a fairly isolated part of the park, when I noticed a young man down near the bridge, just sort of milling around. I don't often meet other people on this trail, and those I do meet seem to be on the move, just as I am. He was looking up the side of the ridge at me while I was descending to the stream and bridge. He looked college age—some sort of pleasant, just OK looking guy with dark features, curly black hair, about 5 feet 10—my height, eyeglasses. My mind said local university, helped, I'm sure because he was wearing a university-logo T-shirt (but, then, so was I).

When I was about down to the bridge, he smiled and said it was a nice day for a hike, and was that what I was out here for? I agreed that was why I was here. (It seemed fairly obvious; this was a hiking trail and I wasn't tuned into other possibilities.) As I got up to him, he pointed to my T-shirt and asked if I'd gone to the football game Saturday night. I said no, but I'd listened to it on the radio. We exchanged a few pleasantries about the game—our university had won in the last second by one point when the opponents failed to convert a touchdown extra point. He seemed to want to chat, but I was hiking, so I moved on.

About ten minutes later, I encountered him again where trails intersected. I'd taken the long route; he'd taken the short. He had stripped off his T and was sitting on a fallen tree. Big smile, pretty good musculature. He asked again whether I was only there to hike. I was starting to get the message and answered that, yes, that was all I'd come to do and what else would there to be to do on a hiking trail in the woods? Well, there's sex, he answered, and gave me "that look" up and down. Then he said he'd be moving off "there" in the woods, and if I was interested, I could follow him.

Now, I don't get all that much now (but some: *grin*) and have been thinking a lot about sex recently. So, I thought, what the hell. And I followed him into the woods. He went straight for a secluded spot, well away from the trails and near the shore of the town's reservoir. He obviously had picked the spot out already. There was a big fallen tree there where you had to perch up just a little to sit. He laid his shirt on top of this and then turned to me as I approached, and I just went into his arms. He stripped my shirt off and laid it on the fallen tree with his and then we did some kissing and chest rubbing and hand exploring. He pushed my shorts and briefs down and off and I did the same for him, and then we did some more kissing and rubbing together of tits and navels and cocks. We both murmured that we liked what we found. Kept our voices down, because, although we probably wouldn't be seen, we likely could have been heard at some distance, especially with the lake so nearby.

This was going on for a while, and I was wondering who was supposed to fuck who here. It had been so long since there hadn't been clear signals on that before we got to this stage from someone I was with. Funny what people think and worry about in these situations. But he then knelt and started sucking me off, which made me decide he was expecting to do me, saving his hardening for right before the fuck. He was good at cocksucking and wouldn't stop until I had creamed his tonsils. Then he stood and pushed me down on my knees and I worked him until he was hard. He had a nice piece; not as long and thick as mine, I don't think, but nice enough anyway.

When it was obvious that we were getting to the fuck part—he had lifted me and turned me toward the fallen tree—I let him know he'd have to use a condom and that I didn't have one. (I just went out that day for an exercise hike.) He'd come prepared with condoms and KY, though, so that part was taken care of. I went belly down on the tree on top of our Ts, with my legs out wide and my hands holding my butt cheeks open, and he put his face into my crack. He was good at this too. Then the KY and a some finger fucking and then the real thing. He just slid on in without any trouble. Nothing exotic—other than being outdoors and a surprise—but nice all the same. He held me with hands on my shoulders and pushed hard with his hips in the thrusts. Half way through the fuck, I did get him to turn me, saying I wanted to watch what he was doing, and he got my butt up on the tree and his cock buried again. His arms went under my thighs, holding them out, and then around to my back and he held his hands together in a locked fist at the small of my back. After getting jolted there back and forth by his short thrusts and my counterthrusts with our eyes locked closely together for a while, I was able to arch back and grab a few saplings at each side to hold myself and he took longer and faster strokes.

After he'd jacked off inside me, he pulled my chest up to his, one arm around me, and stroked me off again between our bellies with the other hand. Nice enough not just to fuck and leave me. Did lip work for a couple of minutes after I'd shot off. Said it was very nice and asked if we could exchange e-mails and meet again—but I told him I didn't do this regularly and already had a steady. But that maybe we'd run across each other in the woods again someday. It would be another couple of weeks before that park came up again in my hike rotation; I did tell him when it would be likely I'd be hiking there again.

It's been a couple of weeks now. And that park is coming up in my rotation and I can make it there on the day I told him I might be there. I am wondering . . .

Chapter Twenty-Four: Like Father Like Son

As I walked into the city on the main street, Damrak, leading directly from Amsterdam's central train station, I nervously fingered the folded e-mail I'd been carrying tucked in my wallet for the past month and a half. Damrak changed into Rokin, and at the end of canal off the Amstel River, I made a right onto Heiligeweg.

I had thought of this possibility on and off for the whole cruise down the Rhine from Mainz to Amsterdam, but I hadn't really taken the chance it would work out as having the whisper of a prayer. We were at the end of our cruise and—magically—the opportunity had just clicked into place. We had a free afternoon in Amsterdam; our ship was docked right next to the Central Station, well within walking distance of the center of the city; and my wife had declared that she was off on a shopping spree with other women from the cruise and that I jolly well could find something to entertain myself for the afternoon.

Little did she know just how right she was.

I hadn't had an encounter with another man the entire two weeks of the voyage, and I was pent up with confused urges—I wanted to take someone and at the same time I also wanted to be taken. I'd been cooped up on a luxury river boat with a gaggle of aging widows too long. I needed release. And now all of the opportunities had fallen into place.

I passed the Bloemen Markt—the area of the morning wholesale flower market—and crossed two canals, and there, just as the e-mail had told me, was Kerkstraat and the prominent sign for Thermos, the renowned gay bar and sauna. I'd been able to tell for several streets that I was in the center of gay life in Amsterdam.

I stood there and swallowed hard. Until now I'd told myself I was just checking out where Cowboy's son's club was. I'd even decided I would have innocently passed by here if my wife and I had taken a walk through the streets of Amsterdam this afternoon—just to be able to tell Cowboy I had seen his son's place. My wife had voiced interest in seeing the red light district, which stretched between here and where the ship was docked, so continuing on to here would seem natural enough, and I could plausibly claim I didn't even know about this section of the city.

Cowboy was a legend in Bangkok, where we had twice lived before. He was an imposing and charismatic black former professional U.S. basketballer who had run afoul of the law and retreated to Thailand, where he had opened a chain of highly successful bars catering to the whole range of preferences—as he himself had done. He and I had had our moments in which he had demonstrated that the whispered claim that he had the biggest cock in Thailand could be credibly defended. But my wife had also known him as well, as he was one of the stars of the embassy bowling league and was celebrated throughout the international community in Thailand for his good humor and generosity in charity work.

We had continued to correspond over the years, and when our Christmas letter for this past year had informed him we were taking a Christmas and New Years cruise down the Rhine, ending in Amsterdam, Cowboy had messaged me that a son he'd sired on a Dutch woman, one of many by-blows, I was sure, owned and operated a gay club in the city and would, Cowboy was sure, love to meet and accommodate me. The son had had enough success as a middle-weight boxer in Europe that he'd managed to follow his father's footsteps as a club owner. I was sure there would be no opportunity to follow up on Cowboy's invitation, but I had folded the e-mail and stowed it away in my wallet and then just put the whole matter in the back of my mind.

But here I was. The e-mail had told me the club, named Chester's, the son's first name, could be found just steps from Thermos on Kerkstraat—and here, by the alignment of the stars and thanks to two weeks on a ship with people reminding me how fleeting life and desirability were, I stood, conflicted. I knew what I wanted, but I had resolved to behave myself on this vacation.

It wouldn't hurt just to see what kind of place the son had, though. I walked more than a block beyond Thermos but saw no evidence of the club. Almost relieved, I retraced my steps, ready to return to the ship. I'd let Cowboy know I looked for the club but couldn't find it.

And then the sign materialized as I got closer to Thermos. It didn't look like a club, though—more like a storefront gay porn shop specializing in magazines, videos, and DVDs. I went in just to make sure, asking the heavily tattooed and pierced clerk behind the register whether this was where the Chester Club was supposed to be. He assured me I was in the right place and guided me to the back of the shop, pulling aside a beaded curtain and ushering me into a small bar area that probably looked a lot better at night, filled with young men, than it did empty in the middle of the afternoon.

There was, however, a good-looking, well-built guy behind the bar, cleaning glasses, who seemed to know who I was when I asked him if Chester was around and that his father in Bangkok had suggested I look him up. The young man poured me a beer and showed me to a nearby banquette.

While I waited for whatever would happen next, a few middle-aged men drifted through, entering from the shop area through the beaded curtain and disappearing through another curtained door on the opposite wall.

The beer half gone, two men materialized from this second doorway. One, the bartender, returned to his duties and soon brought two more beers over to the banquette. The other young man, however, took my breath away. It was almost as if I had been transported back more than two decades in time. The man who came over to my table was a near duplicate of the Cowboy I had known, locked in the time when we both were twenty-five years younger. But he was even more studly than I remembered his father as having been. He was heavily muscled in keeping with his boxing background in contrast to his father's thinner stature and greater height, and he benefited from the softer features and color that came from the mixed American black and Dutch parentage. Chester had the same open, winning smile that served his father so well, though. And he was just as charismatic and welcoming as his father was.

We sat for a good half an hour, talking of his father and of Bangkok and of the son's life in Europe as well. It was clear that Cowboy hadn't just abandoned the son that he no doubt had so casually sired. And it was equally clear that the son worshipped the father. Chester's mannerisms and expressions were honestly inherited from the father, and I found myself beginning to ache for him as I had for his father decades earlier. Memories of his father's legendary cock working inside me flooded into my consciousness, and I was becoming quite horny.

While we talked, a few more men entered from the shop door and exited directly through the door at the rear. I watched this progression and my curiosity was piqued. Chester discerned not only that I was curious but also that I was in the need of attention. I have no doubt that when Cowboy informed his son that an old friend from Bangkok might be coming by, he had clearly spelled out the nature and extent of our friendship.

"Would you care to come back through that door those men have entered?" Chester asked me. "I think you might enjoy what we have back there."

I would have followed Chester anywhere at this point. The room he then took me into was darker than the club area, at least the half of the room he sat me in. The other half of the room, which was behind what might have been a one-sided glass window, was brightly lit. It was lined with a rich, blue velvet material—floor, walls, and ceiling—and there were divans of the same blue velvet scattered about on three levels rising to the back of the room. And draped on these divans were nearly a dozen naked, handsome young men, easily discoursing with each other, not paying any attention to what was happening on the dimly lit side of the glass.

Two of the men I had just previously seen entering this room while I was talking and drinking beer with Chester in the bar area were deep in conversation and negotiation with another man, who obviously was some sort of host. As I watched, fascinated, the host picked up a wall phone. All of the naked young men looked over toward what appeared to be a speaker hanging on the wall, and a young blond smiled to the others, rose and blew them kisses, and exited through a door at the side of the room. One of the men on this side of the glass was ushered out of a door on the same side of the room. It didn't require much of my imagination to figure out what business was being conducted in this room.

"Do you see anything you like?" Chester asked me. "I can offer you any of these young men for half price—which we mark in these little packets." He held up silver-foil packets of condoms. "Because you are a friend of my father's, I can waive the house fee. It wouldn't be fair to waive the young man's fee as well, though. I apologize for that, but I'm sure you understand. For you, it would be 50 euros for one packet and another 25 for each succeeding one. More than three, though, and you would have to make an additional selection and pay the base 50 euro-fee again. I'm sure you can understand the need for that as well. We can't work our boys too hard. And for you, we needn't talk about session time limits. Are you interested? I would be very pleased to accommodate you."

My head was reeling. I'd never paid for sex before in my life and vowed I never would. But the circumstances were compelling here. Not only was my need great—and quite obvious to Chester as I watched the luscious young men on the other side of the glass move languidly around—but it also would be an insult to both father and son, I thought, if I refused the offer. Still, my mind was racing to surface all of the reasons to chicken out.

"They look so young," I said. "Too young."

"Ahh. This is Amsterdam," Chester said softly. "The age of consent in the Netherlands is sixteen, not eighteen as it is in the United States."

A mixture of relief and regret flooded into my body and the tension began to flow out. This was my out. I didn't have to fight farther with my demons.

"I am an American," I said, trying to fill my voice with regret. "I can't forget U.S. guidelines and I must admit that I agree with them. I just couldn't manage with the younger age, I'm afraid."

"That needn't be a problem," Chester countered smoothly. "That one and that one are over eighteen. Does either one appeal?" He had pointed them out by name, but I was too nervous and discombobulated by the situation to retain the names.

I was trapped. I looked at both of the young men he pointed out, and although they both, indeed, appealed to me, a willowy redheaded youth arrested my attention. I had wanted to fuck a man for days, and my attention had latched onto one of the waiters on the ship as my fantasy partner. There was enough of a similarity between the youth being offered to me here and the waiter of my fantasies that my juices started to flow and desire and the heat of animal rut began to push out all of my reasoning to the contrary. As my desire for the young man rose, however, it fought with an overriding desire for Chester himself. I couldn't help but wonder if he was as masterful a top as his father had been. But Chester hadn't offered himself, so I did what I could to concentrate on the redhead.

Clearly pleased both with my choice and that I had chosen—and that I had bought two packets—Chester led me through a door while the young man was called forth and exited from the glassed room. We met in the hallway beyond the room. Chester said something to the young man in Dutch, and the young man smiled shyly at me—his expression one of complete openness and willingness. Either he was a consummate actor or he was pleased with what he saw in me, an attitude that heightened my desire for him.

Leaving Chester behind, the young man preceded me up two narrow flights of stairs. Watching his butt cheeks tighten and loosen as we went up the stairs, I couldn't help myself—I reached between his legs from in back and caressed his cock, which began to fill out. He turned to me with a smile, and we engaged in our first tender kiss there on the stairs before he turned and climbed more slowly now, his thighs bowed out around my invading hand.

From the third floor landing, we entered a small, but well-appointed bed chamber with a double bed in the center and mirrors on all walls and the ceiling over the bed. A small bath with a shower was located through another door in the wall. Immediately upon entering the room, the young man slowly undressed me, and we engaged in some lip work and hand exploration before he led me into the bath and we showered together. He soaped me and then knelt and sucked me to fullness in the shower. He opened the first packet and crowned my cock, and I spent my initial 50 euros taking him, both of us standing, from the rear against the Dutch tiles of the shower under a fine misting of water.

He was well-schooled in his trade and made me feel like I was taking a fresh, yet willing, virgin for the first time.

When he had come for me and I had come in him, he rolled the condom off me, disposed of it, and then soaped and rinsed me off again. He then toweled me and I stood there and watched and reloaded as he put on a show while he toweled himself off.

When I was engorging again, he went over to the bed and sat at the foot of the mattress, laid back on the bed, spread his legs, and raised his arms in a come-hither motion.

I came hither and hunched over him. We kissed as he played with my nipples and I with his. As my cock stiffened, he widened and raised his legs farther and I rubbed my cock up and down in his ass crack and across his puckered hole and began and increasingly intrusive and frenzied dance of rubbing along his hole and poking at it with my prick.

He was moaning and writhing under me, giving a good show of wanting and needing what I had to give him but being fearful to give up his "virginity." I'd never had this feeling of taking a young man for the first time again and again before, and it was driving me wild. He barely had time to roll the second condom on me before I was thrusting myself inside him, taking him with vigor and a force that I could no longer control.

He was arching his back and bucking against me and crying out his ravishment so loudly that I didn't hear Chester enter the room until I felt his strong hands on my hips. I looked around in surprise, not being able to turn really, because my cock was buried in the redhead's ass to the hilt, but Chester pulled away enough for me to see that he was only wearing a condom.

He was even more magnificent and muscle-hard than I had remembered his father to be, and what he was swinging between his legs rivaled his father and would make the old man proud. He was a beautiful, glistening, hard chocolate brown, and my knees went weak at the sight of him.

He covered me closely from behind, his cock running up the small of my back, and after kissing me possessively on the lips when I turned my head to him, he nuzzled the hollow of my neck with his lips and whispered in my ear that what he was going to give me was a present from his father—in memory of our good times together. Then he knelt behind me and worked my asshole with his tongue as he guided my stroking inside the redhead with his beefy palms on my hips.

It wasn't only the redhead who was sighing and moaning now.

There was no waiting for it when Chester was satisfied with his preparations and stood behind me. He thrust inside me in a long, gliding stroke just as I remembered his father doing, and while he rode me hard and deep, memories of the Cowboy technique flooded in and I writhed and flipped off into a seventh heaven of my own, being barely aware of the warm wetness of the redhead spouting up my belly followed quickly by my own ejaculation. Then the redhead was gone and Chester pushed me up on the bed on my belly, straddled my hips between his strong thighs, pulling my legs together and tightening my ass channel more closely around his thrusting cock—which just kept jack hammering down into me as he pushed down on my shoulders with his hands. I was exhausted when I heard him cry out and felt the condom balloon out with his semen deep inside me.

Chester left me briefly, but then both he and the redhead reappeared and pushed me over on my side. The redheaded youth exchanged my spent condom for a fresh one—which I hadn't purchased. But before I could point that out, he had come down on the bed and nestled his back against my chest and guided my recovered cock inside him from the rear. Then Chester, freshly sheathed, came down behind me, sandwiching me—me sidesplitting the redhead and Chester sidesplitting me—in a languid three-way fuck that lasted for a good half hour.

When I felt I was able to walk again and Chester and I were cooling down with a postcoital beer in now more active bar downstairs, I pointed out that we hadn't settled the bill and that I was quite willing to pay for the extra packets. Chester just laughed, though, and said that he hadn't believed it, but his father had been right—that I had been as entertaining for Chester as he had been asked to be for me and that he'd cover the redhead's fees himself.

It wasn't particularly late, but it was dark as I walked briskly back to the ship through streets of the red light district of Amsterdam—paying no attention to the undulations and invitations of the scantily, black-laced-clad women in the glass windows. My thoughts were still in the thrall of the Cowboy and Chester duo. Like father like son—and a very good like it was.

Chapter Twenty-Five: Uncertain Arrival

I see him coming out of the passageway from the plane, another one sent to me from the Levant to acclimate to living in the States in exchange for pleasuring me. He's everything I had been told to expect: big, tall—more than six and a half feet, I think—and thick of body but in a well-cut, all power and muscle way. Big hands, big feet, bulging biceps, a T-shirt just bursting with chest muscle.

He isn't smiling; he looks tired. I worry what he'll think when he sees me; whether he hoped I'd be younger or as massive as he is. But then he sees me, obviously recognizing me from photos, and his face lights up in a broad grin. He's different from the last one, who was thin and serious, but who both beefed up and lightened up under my tutelage. I hoped this one wasn't as timid as the first. We lost so much time in the beginning, time that we both wished we had when we at last parted.

He wants to hug me when he reaches me, a bear hug, as if we are long-lost relatives. I grunt, as I realize that he's using the closeness as an excuse to take my hand and put it on his basket. He's ready for action, obviously, and wants me to know it. And I gasp at the size of him. He touches me unobtrusively, but intimately, as we move toward the baggage belts. On the escalator, he's close behind me and he reaches around me with a big hand and pushes his mitt up under my shirt and palms my belly. He's been instructed well. If I wasn't already melting, I would be now. My hand is trembling on the escalator's plastic handrail. My breath begins to become ragged. I'm not sure how I'll be able to wait until we get to the hotel, even though I selected one very close to the airport.

But I don't have to wait. At baggage claim, a message is flashing above the conveyor belts that the baggage has been delayed.

He asks me where the men's room is. I point to one and say I'll wait in case his bags appear, asking him what they look like. He smiles and tells me the bags can wait—that we can't fuck if I'm not in the men's room with him. He's said it in a conversational, natural tone. I glance around as surreptitiously as I can to see if anyone's heard what he said. No one seems to have; they are all chattering to each other, not zeroing in on any specific conversation other than their own. I flash him a warning look, and his eyes turn to those of a wounded teddy bear.

My knees are like rubber as we walk over to the men's room. What seemed so close a minute ago now seems miles away. Surely everyone we pass knows what we are going to do in there—or are thinking of doing. I'm not at all sure I can go through with this.

We reach the door to the men's room and I falter. But he just passes on beside me and through the door. So I follow. It's a large one, with the shiny steel-sided stalls in banks in a compartment behind the room with the urinals and wash basins.

He selects a stall nearly all the way at the end of the row and pulls me in with him, turns me, and dives for my lips with his. His hands go to encase my buns, and he pulls my package into his. I can feel the urging and heat of him. He smells like cedar and cinnamon, fresh from the Levant. He takes his hands back, but only long enough to unbuckle himself and open his fly and push his briefs down. Then they are back on my buns. But this time I have unbuckled myself, and my pants pull apart and sink down my legs as his hands go inside my briefs and encase me again, skin on skin. A long, fat finger is already reaching for my hole. He grinds my pelvis against his, and I arch back and moan, feeling my manhood against his, his a veritable throbbing club of readiness. My hands go to him and I gasp at his size and urgency. Big hands, big feet, gigantic penis—wanting me, just as I have wanted what he has to give me for months since I sent his predecessor away in this very airport.

He turns me roughly and makes me lean across the toilet, my legs spread on either side of the seat, my hand clutching at the tank top. My pants are stripped off and slung over my head onto the top of the tank top. I lay my cheek on top of the trousers and try not to cry out as he attacks my anus with his searching mouth and tongue and long, thick fingers. Then he's crouched over me and is entering me and entering me and entering. Thrusting and withdrawing and then thrusting again, deeper. Breathing heavily, both of us. We hear men, in conversation, entering the men's room. And my Lebanese lover lifts my legs off the floor, with strong hands under my thighs, helping me wedge my feet in the corners where the stall walls meet the back wall.

Crouching below me on massive thighs now, miles and miles of rock-hard, throbbing cock pointed straight up inside my hole. Lifting me and sinking me down on his possessing rod, finding every inch of me inside, stretching me, worrying my canal, coaxing it to expand for him, to take more of him in with each lifting and sinking. My legs have leverage against the wall now, none of me showing below the edge of the stall. One of his hands goes to my belly and the other to my throat just below my chin, pulling my head into his face so that he can kiss my ears and cheeks and let me hear the sound of his pent-up need to fuck me. Me providing the piston action now with the stiffening and release of the tense in my leveraged legs. Me fucking myself on his gigantic tool. Screaming and moaning in passion but only on the inside—I hope. Trying my best not to betray our exertions, my briefs stuffed inside my own mouth to aid my attempt at silence.

Then his hands are back on my hips. Jackhammering me up and down, faster and faster, and pulling out farther with each movement and digging deeper with each thrust. He senses I am ready to shoot and then pulls me all the way down, the sensitive skin of my butt cheeks mashing his black, curly pubic hair. He holds for interminable seconds, slowly pulls me back up until I can feel his bulbous glans at my rim—and then a swift death—thrusting me down as he reaches over and flushes the toilet, masking at least partially my involuntary passioned cry of being taken totally as my ejaculate splatters against the cold steel of the toilet.

He comes then inside me as well in a drowning flood. The catch in his breath and slight whimper as he ejaculates tells me that he is mine as much as I am his.

He holds me there, nuzzling my neck with his lips. "How far to this hotel?" he whispers in my ear.

"Not far, not far at all," I whisper back in breathless voice.

"Good," he says. "I want to hear you scream out loud for it now."

I take charge as soon as we've redressed, even though I still feel like Jell-O inside. Telling him to wait a couple of minutes before joining me in baggage claim.

I keep my distance while the bags, at last, are arriving, and I manage to wrap myself in businesslike decorum, with a slightly stern look on my face. He's got that wounded teddy bear look again on his face, not sure if he's done something wrong. I want him on that edge at least until we get to the hotel. I make him carry the heaviest bags to the car and then make him sit in the backseat all the way to the hotel. I've already checked in, so we just breeze past reception, which is too busy to care about us anyway, and go up to the room.

I send him to the shower. He tries to apologize as he strips down, but I tell him just to go.

When he pads back out of the bathroom, stark naked and patting at his wet body with a fluffy towel, I am there, sitting on the end of the bed, legs and arms wide, a big smile on my face.

"Welcome to America," I say. "Come and get me."

"But . . . but . . . ." he stammers, "You aren't mad with me? The car . . ."

"I couldn't trust myself with you in the front seat," I say.

And then he is upon me. No months of breaking down timidness with this one.

About the Author

Habu is one of the pen names of a former supersonic spy jet pilot, intelligence agent, male model, movie actor, and diplomat. A wild youth in South East Asia was spent enjoying whatever sexual opportunities came his way, and much of his gay male writing is about recalling incidents from those days and inventing ones he'd perhaps have liked to experience. He now leads a very quiet and ordinary happily married family life.

An American, he is a published mainstream novelist and short story writer under another name and in another dimension of his life. He has written or cowritten (with Sabb) over 500 published short stories and nearly 100 published erotica e-books, primarily of gay fiction but also memoir, straight fiction and ménage fiction. His hand and creative writing can be seen in stories and books by habu, sr71plt, Dirk Hessian, Shabbu, and Stephen Kessel—among unrevealed others that might surprise readers. The fictionalized GM memoir *Flying High, Diving Deep* is loosely based on his life experiences. He can be found at the adults only gay male site BarbarianSpy, which he shares with Sabb and Dirk Hessian.

Our authors always like to receive feedback, and appreciate it when readers post reviews at Goodreads, Amazon, and other sites.

BarbarianSpy

FOR LITERARY HEAT

Not all books listed below may currently be on release.

BOOKS BY DIRK HESSIAN

The Beautiful Way

Blue and Gray

Colonel's Treasure

Beginning of Time

Prophecy of Noto

The King's Men

Labyrinth

BOOKS BY HABU

Gay Erotica

Memoir Faction

Flying High, Diving Deep

General

Hard Knocks U

Dark Angel Sounding

Man's Man

My Neighbor's Hot Tub

Trip Money

Vortex

Clint Folsom Mysteries Compendium Volume 1

Clint Folsom Mysteries Compendium Volume 2

Grab Bag 1

Grab Bag 2

Across the Threshold

The Indian Doctor

Sailorboy

Home to Fire Island

The Sporting Life

Platres Conclave

Fetish Galore!

Choke Hold

www.ingramcontent.com/pod-product-compliance
Lightning Source LLC
Chambersburg PA
CBHW020438180626
46812CB00003B/1303